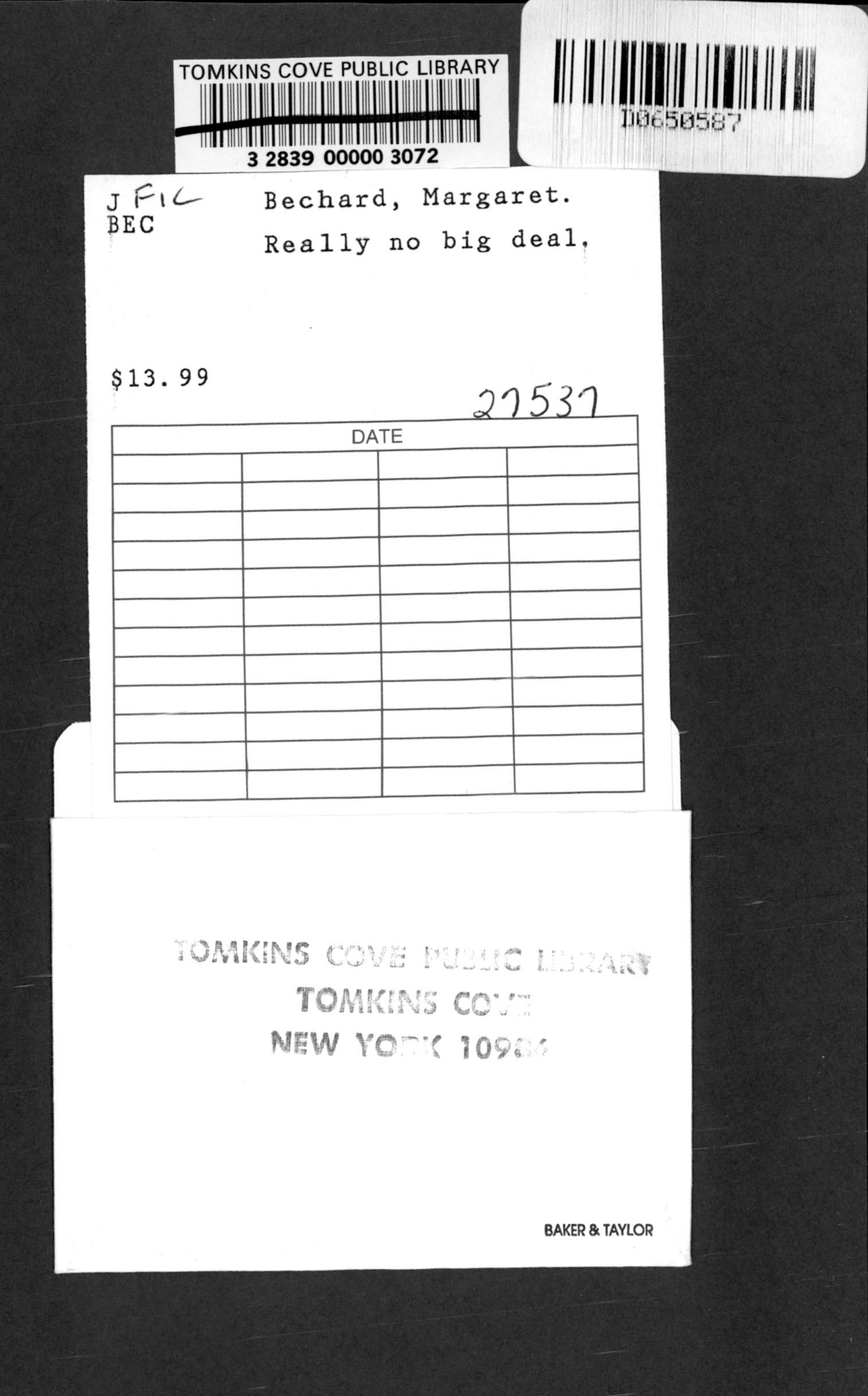
TOMKINS COVE PUBLIC LIBRARY
3 2839 00000 3072
J FIC
BEC
Bechard, Margaret.
Really no big deal.
$13.99
27537
DATE
BAKER & TAYLOR

Really No Big Deal

by Margaret Bechard

VIKING
Published by the Penguin Group
Penguin Books USA Inc., 375 Hudson Street, New York, New York 10014, U.S.A.
Penguin Books Ltd, 27 Wrights Lane, London W8 5TZ, England
Penguin Books Australia Ltd, Ringwood, Victoria, Australia
Penguin Books Canada Ltd, 10 Alcorn Avenue, Toronto, Ontario, Canada M4V 3B2
Penguin Books (N.Z.) Ltd, 182–190 Wairau Road, Auckland 10, New Zealand

Penguin Books Ltd, Registered Offices: Harmondsworth, Middlesex, England

First published in 1994 by Viking, a division of Penguin Books USA Inc.

1 3 5 7 9 10 8 6 4 2

LIBRARY OF CONGRESS CATALOGING-IN-PUBLICATION DATA
Bechard, Margaret E.
Really no big deal / by Margaret Bechard. p. cm.
Summary: Seventh-grader Jonah Truman's main concerns are meeting girls and avoiding the class bully,
until he and his friend Amanda start working as helpers at children's parties
and his mother begins dating the principal of his school.
ISBN 0-670-85444-1
[1. Schools—Fiction. 2. Friendship—Fiction. 3. Moneymaking projects—Fiction.] Title.
PZ7.B38066Re 1994 [Fic]—dc20 93-31065 CIP AC

Printed in U.S.A. Set in 12 Point M Plantin

This book is dedicated to the members of the critique group:
Becky Hickox Ayres,
Susan Fletcher,
David Gifaldi,
Eric Kimmel,
Winifred Morris,
Dorothy Morrison,
Graham Salisbury,
and
Ellen Howard (member-for-life).

"It is not often that someone comes along
who is a true friend and a good writer."

—E. B. White

CONTENTS

"Trust Me, Jonah"...1

Not Funny At All...10

A Piece of Cake...19

Jonah Likes Katherine...28

Worse Than Halloween...37

Going Out...46

Mallory...55

Under the Table...64

Water Fight...74

Just Another Great Day...83

Bob...93

"I Never Thought You Had It in You"...102

Pirates!...111

"What Were You Doing in Here?"...122

Really No Big Deal...132

"Do You Like Amanda?"...142

CHAPTER ONE

"Trust Me, Jonah"

"Hey, Jonah. Wait up!"

I moved out of the stampede of kids heading for freedom and waited for my friend Kevin Martinez.

He waved a paper in my face. "I wanted to show you the flyer."

I shifted my baritone horn case to my other hand and took the paper. "Lawns mowed. Honest, trustworthy, reasonable rates," I read out loud. I looked at Kevin. "It sounds like we're Boy Scouts."

He shrugged. "My mom said we don't want people to think we're ripping them off." He tapped the bottom of the page. "Now I just have to figure out how to center the phone number."

"There is no phone number."

"I know. For some reason, it keeps coming out on the next page. I think it's got something to do with the font I'm using."

"Yeah, yeah," I said. Kevin is my best friend, but he drives me a little crazy when he starts talking technical. I handed the paper back. "It looks good. You did good."

He grinned, one of his big grins that show his retainer. "I figure we can paper the neighborhood with these, and we'll have earned the money for the beach trip by the beginning of June."

I glanced out the window across the hall. A gust of wind peppered the glass with rain and wet leaves. "You don't mow lawns in March in Portland, Oregon."

He waved the paper again. "But we'll be ready!"

The door behind us opened, and Mr. Decker, the principal, came out. He was wearing a gray suit and a purple shirt and a truly ugly red-and-yellow tie. He frowned at us. "You don't want to miss the bus, guys."

"I don't even ride the bus," I muttered to Kevin as we shoved back into the flow of kids.

Travis Hunter bumped me from behind, and my horn case banged into Kevin's leg. "Don't you know why Decker wants us all out of here?" Travis asked. I didn't say anything, but Travis told us anyway. "He has the hots for McNeal!"

Travis turned and poked Jerry Fitzner, who was walking on his other side. Jerry laughed, a loud and obnoxious laugh, and then they both shoved in between Kevin and me and headed for the door.

"What a pair of jerks," Kevin said.

I glanced back to see if Mr. Decker had heard, but he'd disappeared already.

Kevin and I pushed through the big front doors. The cold air felt good. The school buses were pulled up at the curb, and the smell of diesel fuel mixed with the drizzle and wet pavement. Kids were milling all over the place. Two sixth graders were chasing each other around one of the posts, and Mr. Adamson was clapping his hands and saying, "Boys, boys!"

Kevin stuffed the flyer under my arm. "I know we'll get plenty of jobs, Jonah," he said. "I'll see you tomorrow."

I stuffed the flyer into my backpack, turned up the collar of my jacket, and started down the side-walk. I had to dodge two kids on their bicycles and a bunch of eighth graders who were imitating Mr. Adamson behind his back. I passed a clump of girls, and Amanda Matzinger fell into step be-side me.

"Well, if it isn't the mayor of Munchkinland," she said, but quietly so nobody else could hear.

"And if it isn't the Jolly Green Giant," I said.

She grinned and pulled her long, dark hair out of her collar. I guess you could say that, if she weren't a girl, Amanda would be my best friend, too. We've lived next door to each other just about all of our lives. We even went to the same preschool, and my mother has some pictures of us playing in the sprinkler that I plan to destroy when I can get my hands on them.

We walked down the line of buses. Jerry stuck his head out of a window and shouted, "Hey, Truman! Why don't you just get into the horn case and let Moose Matzinger carry you home?"

"Get a life, Fitzner!" Amanda shouted, and Jerry laughed that laugh again.

I ducked my face further down into my jacket. My mother kept telling me that any day now I'd experience this great growth spurt. So far, all I'd gotten out of adolescence was zits. And Amanda, who'd been tall enough to begin with, just kept getting taller and taller. Life is not fair.

Mr. Decker must have doubled around and come out the back door because he was standing at the head of the line of buses with Miss McNeal. She said something, and Mr. Decker put his head back and laughed. "Hi, Mr. Decker," Amanda said as we went by.

"Hi, Amanda. Have a nice afternoon." Mr. Decker smiled, and Miss McNeal waved.

Amanda leaned her head down by my ear. "Don't they make a cute couple?"

"You and Travis," I said. I glanced back. "He's way too old for her."

Amanda shook her head. "No. He just looks

that way, I think. A bunch of us were talking about it before fitness, and we decided he's prematurely gray."

"You guys sit around and talk about Mr. Decker?"

Amanda shrugged. "Most of the girls think he's very cute."

"Cute? He's got a huge nose."

"It's an interesting nose."

I snorted and shifted the horn case to my other hand.

Amanda looked down at me. "Speaking of cute, what were you and Kevin talking about back there?"

"You think Kevin's cute, too?"

"Oh, yeah. All the girls do. That dark curly hair. Those big brown eyes. That saxophone." She sighed a big, fake sigh, like she was only kidding.

I shook my head. And here I'd been thinking that Kevin was sort of just a little bit of a nerd.

Amanda poked me with her elbow. "They think you're cute, too, Jonah."

"All the girls?" I wanted to ask about Katherine Chang specifically, but I couldn't.

"Well . . ." Amanda grinned. "Let's just say a large number of the girls. So, what were you and Kevin talking about?"

"Nothing." I was still wondering who exactly thought I was cute. "He has this idea for mowing lawns. To raise some money for the trip to Astoria."

"You're going, aren't you?"

I nodded. "I'm pretty sure. I just have to earn some of the money myself."

Amanda sighed. "I know. Me, too. My parents think it will make the whole thing more educational. As if going to the beach for the weekend is supposed to be educational."

"Well, we are going to look at tide pools and go to the maritime museum."

"But there'll be lots of time left over." Amanda moved over so Pam Avery could get by on her skateboard. I moved over, too, so I wouldn't bump into Amanda. Feeling funny about bumping into girls, even girls like Amanda, is another of the great side effects of adolescence.

"Anyway, I have to pay for all my extras. Souvenirs and postcards and lunches and stuff like that. That's why I need to talk to you." She was staring straight ahead, watching Pam dodging down the sidewalk.

I frowned at her. "What's this got to do with me?"

"Well, I have this idea, too. A business idea." She glanced at me and then looked away again.

I groaned. "Oh, no," I said. "Not another

surefire, money-making business idea." Ever since our first lemonade stand, back in kindergarten, Amanda has been coming up with ideas to make money. Ideas that always seem to involve me. I think maybe it's because she's an only child. "No way am I washing dogs. Or painting mailboxes."

"No, no. This is nothing like that. This is very easy and very clean." She turned toward me. "Trust me, Jonah."

"Trust you," I said, and my voice sort of went high and squeaky. "The last time I let you talk me into one of your crazy ideas, I ended up wet and filthy, and I owed my mom twenty bucks for a new pair of jeans."

Amanda was shaking her head. "This is different," she said. "This is an absolute gold mine." She leaned a little closer, like she was going to divulge state secrets or something. "I have one word for you, Jonah. Birthday parties."

"That's two words," I said. She just raised her eyebrows and didn't say anything. A bus went past us. Two kids had their noses and mouths pressed flat against the glass of the back window.

"All right. I give up," I said. "How do you make money from birthday parties?"

"We help the mothers, see? With the entertainment and games and . . . and . . ." Amanda waved her free hand. "And stuff."

"And I suppose I get to wear the clown suit," I said.

She sighed. "Jonah Truman. You are so suspicious. Mrs. Norton has all this stuff figured out."

"Mrs. Norton? Who's Mrs. Norton?"

"This friend of my mom's. All we have to do is run the games and keep the kids from wrecking the house. We're talking an hour—an hour and a half tops."

"How old are these kids? Not that I'm thinking about doing it," I added, fast.

"Mrs. Norton said Tiffany's going to be seven."

My little sister, Liz, had been seven last year. "Forget it," I said.

"Oh, come on, Jonah. Mrs. Norton's going to be there. And Mr. Norton. Mrs. Norton needs our help because Mr. Norton has to run the video camera." She poked my shoulder. "They're going to pay us five dollars each. For a measly hour, Jonah."

I thought about that. Mom paid me a buck fifty to baby-sit Liz for an hour. I made more mowing lawns, but I couldn't count on that for a long time. "Why don't you ask Shawna or Jill to do it?"

"I just thought I'd ask you first. I mean, I thought you might need the money." She squinted up into the drizzle.

"I do need the money," I said.

"Well, then." Amanda stopped and I stopped, too. "I really need your help, Jonah." I noticed that some of her mascara had smudged down onto her cheek. "Besides, I already sort of told Mrs. Norton you'd do it."

"Amanda!"

"Well, I couldn't believe you'd be so dumb you'd turn down five bucks just for going to a party. It'll be a piece of cake." She laughed and punched me on the shoulder. "Come on. Be a good guy."

I rubbed my shoulder. "You promise, no dogs and no paint?"

"Cross my heart." She made the gesture to go with the promise, which sort of embarrassed me.

"One party," I said, and I held up one finger. I knew the way Amanda's mind worked.

"One party," she said. She turned and started walking again.

I shook my head and started after her. "Why," I muttered, "do I know I'm going to regret this?"

CHAPTER TWO

Not Funny At All

"So how was school today, Jonah?" Mom crunched down on a carrot stick and looked at me across the table. The woman spends all day with twenty-five fourth graders. You'd think school would be the last thing she'd want to talk about.

"Fine," I said.

"How did the algebra test go?"

"Fine." I scooped up a couple of fish sticks and dumped them onto my plate.

"And the social studies presentation?"

"Fine."

She sighed. "Does *anything* interesting ever happen in the seventh grade?"

I thought about telling her that I'd done the presentation with Katherine Chang, and I'd gotten so nervous I'd nearly put out my eye with my pencil. I thought about telling her the dirty joke Travis Hunter told everybody in the locker room after intramurals. I thought about telling her how Jerry Fitzner had humiliated me in front of busloads of kids. Instead I said, "No. Nothing interesting."

She sighed. "How was your day, Liz?"

"Well . . ." My little sister leaned forward and put her sleeve right in her tartar sauce. "James fell down at recess and had to get two Band-Aids. Anne got sent to the office for burping. And the goldfish died."

Mom nodded. She looked at me. "See, Jonah? See how Liz can tell us about her day in third grade?"

"Mother. If everybody who burped in middle school got sent to the office, half the kids would be in there every day. And we'd just dissect the goldfish." I plunged my fork into a fish stick and waggled my eyebrows at Liz.

"You can't dissect our goldfish. Mr. McKenzie flushed it down the toilet." She stuck a forkful of peas in her mouth, chewed, and opened her mouth so I could see.

Ever since she was born, people have said how much Liz and I look alike, mostly, I guess, because we have the same straight brown hair and the same blue eyes. And we're both not exactly big people. Nothing makes your day like having somebody say, "Oh, you look just like your little sister."

"You cooked a great dinner, Liz," Mom said. "These are the best fish sticks I've had since—"

"Last Tuesday," I said. I poked one. "I think these *are* the fish sticks we had last Tuesday."

"Jonah," Mom said.

Liz stuck her tongue out at me. I poured ketchup all over my fish. I studied the effect, then poured some more over my peas. "Why can't we have hamburgers? Or that Stroganoff stuff you make?"

"It's the end of the month, Jonah," Mom said. "This is an end-of-the-month dinner." She reached out and grabbed another handful of carrots.

"Is that all you're eating?" I said. "You aren't dieting again, are you?"

Liz groaned.

"I had a fish stick," Mom smiled at Liz. "The best one I've had all week. Now I'm filling up on vegetables."

I narrowed my eyes at her. "Ms. Perkins read us this thing in homeroom today."

"Aha! Something did happen at school!"

"It was all about the dangers of dieting." I pointed at her. "Ms. Perkins said we should learn to accept our bodies the way they are."

Mom made a face. "That," she said, "is easy for Beth Perkins to say."

I nodded and bit into a carrot. I hadn't really believed it either.

"I like you just the way you are, Mom," Liz said.

Mom laughed. "Thank you, sweetie."

"We got a letter from Dad," Liz said. "He says he's fine, and Maureen's fine, and the baby's sleeping through the night."

Mom stopped laughing. "Well. That does sound fine." I looked at her and decided there was maybe a fifty percent chance she actually meant it.

"Speaking of Dad," I said, and I stirred my peas around in the ketchup, "did you ask him about the money?"

Mom laughed and took a bite of a carrot stick. It snapped under her teeth. "What money in particular do you mean?"

"Mom!" I looked up at her. "The money for the class trip to the beach. You said you'd ask him if he could help out."

Mom shoved her hair off her forehead, which is a sign that she's getting ticked off. "You could ask him yourself, you know, Jonah."

I watched the red ketchup swirl into the green peas. "I think it would be better if you asked him."

She snorted. I made a mental note never to snort at my kids. "I will ask him, Jonah. I said I'd ask him and I'll ask him. He has a lot of expenses right now, you know."

"Yeah, I know." I stuck a forkful of fish into my mouth and chewed. It tasted awful.

"I thought you and Kevin were going to try to figure out a way to make some money."

"We are, Mom. Kevin's doing this flyer thing on his computer that we can pass around the neighborhood to get lawn mowing jobs but . . ." I pointed out the window. "There's not a lot of lawn mowing right now."

"The daffodils are out," Liz said.

Mom and I both ignored her. "And," I said, "I've got this job with Amanda. We're working at a birthday party this weekend, helping with the games and stuff."

"Whose birthday?" Liz asked.

"I don't know. Some kid named Tiffany Norton, I guess."

"I know Tiffany Norton. I hate Tiffany Norton."

"Well, you don't have to be there."

"Just don't get paint on your clothes," Mom said. "Remember the last time you worked with Amanda."

"I know, I know." I drove a fish stick through the ketchup and stuck the whole thing into my mouth.

Mom picked up another carrot. "Do you have a lot of homework tonight?"

I shook my head. "Algebra," I mumbled around the mouthful of food. "Why?"

"Well, you could start making some money. I need a baby-sitter."

Liz moaned and flopped back in her chair.

"Do you have to go to another meeting? I hate it when you go to meetings."

"Actually . . ." Mom wrinkled up her nose and her mouth. "I guess I'm sort of going out on a date." She looked at us like she thought maybe we were going to laugh.

We didn't. Liz raised her eyebrows, and I frowned. Mom and Dad had been divorced for two years, and Mom had never gone out on anything she'd called a date.

"Who with?" I asked.

"Well . . ." She seemed to be very interested in the carrot stick. "I know you're going to think this is funny, Jonah."

Right away, I knew I wasn't going to think it was funny at all.

"I'm going out with Mr. Decker."

"Who?"

"Mr. Decker," Mom said. "Bob Decker? The principal at your school."

"I know who he is," I said. "I know who Mr. Decker is!" I guess my voice was getting a little loud, because Liz put her hands over her ears. "You can't go out with Mr. Decker."

Mom looked surprised. "Why not?"

"Because . . . because . . ." There had to be a good reason. "Because you don't even know him," I said.

"Yes I do, Jonah. He's on that school reform

committee I'm on. After the last couple of meetings, we've gone out for coffee, and he's called a couple of times and . . . well . . ."

"Isn't he too old for you?" I said.

Mom laughed. "Why, thank you, Jonah."

I thought about Mr. Decker and his bushy gray hair and his big nose. I thought about the way he sort of hung out in the halls between classes, checking to see if anybody was goofing off. I thought about him sort of hanging out in the halls of my house. I ran my hand through my hair, which makes it look really stupid, but I couldn't help it.

"Don't you think you're overreacting just a little bit?" Mom asked.

"You put your sleeve in your ketchup," Liz said.

I looked down. She was right. "Mom," I said. I made my voice as deep and serious as I could. "You can't do this to me."

"We're just going out, Jonah. Believe me. This is no big deal."

"What if somebody from school sees you?" That would be a really big deal. All I would need was somebody from school seeing my mom out on a date with the principal.

She shook her head and laughed. "I'll tell you what. If we see anybody you know, I'll put my popcorn bucket over my head."

Liz laughed. "Where are you going to go?"

"To a movie," Mom said.

"What are you going to wear?"

"I thought I'd just wear what I have on."

"Oh, I think you should dress up," Liz said. "I think you should wear the dress you wore to Aunt Monica's wedding."

"She looks fine," I said. I knew what Mr. Decker would be wearing. One of those gray suits and one of those ugly ties. Either that or he'd have on the red sweater with the buttons up the front.

Mom reached over and touched my arm. Her hand felt dry and warm. "It's just one date, honey," she said.

"It's a school night," I said. "I don't think either one of you should be going out on a school night."

Mom slid her chair back and stood up. "We'll be home early. I promise." She patted my shoulder as she went by. "He should be here in a few minutes. I'm going to put on some lipstick."

"Lipstick! You don't need lipstick!" I said, but she was already gone.

Liz stood up and started clearing the table. "I think it's nice she's going out. It'll make Grandma really happy."

I grabbed her arm. "You don't need to tell Grandma. In fact, you don't need to tell anybody!"

"You're not the boss, Jonah." She pulled her arm free. "I think you're acting really dumb."

"Yeah, well, how would you feel if Mom was going out with the principal of your school?"

Liz laughed. "Mom wouldn't go out with Mrs. Reinhard."

"Consider yourself lucky." I got up and started loading the dishwasher.

Liz handed me a dripping plate. "Have you ever been sent to the principal's office?"

"No." I looked at her. "Have you?"

She shook her head. "Principals," she said, "can be kind of scary."

"No kidding," I said.

I jammed the last dish into the dishwasher and headed upstairs to my room. Winifred and Dorothy, my hamsters, were scurrying around in their cage, revving up for the night. I got out my horn and started practicing.

I picked a nice, loud piece to practice. I didn't hear the doorbell ring. I didn't hear Mom talking to Mr. Decker. I didn't even hear her shout good-bye up the stairs.

After a few minutes, Liz stuck her head in my door. "You can come out now. It's safe."

I ignored her and went right on playing.

CHAPTER THREE

A Piece of Cake

Mr. Decker called on Saturday morning and invited us all to go to the art museum with him. I was really glad I had to go to work with Amanda.

Mrs. Matzinger dropped us off at the Nortons' house, and we walked up to the front door together. Amanda was wearing a sweater and a short jeans skirt. I was wearing my new jeans and this shirt I hate, because Mom had said nobody goes to a job or a birthday party dressed like a slob.

Before we could ring the doorbell, the door swung open, and a blast of noise hit us. "Thank goodness you're here," Mrs. Norton said, and she grabbed us both and pulled us into the house. "Some of the guests arrived a little early, and I'm afraid they're getting rambunctious."

The living room was packed with little girls, all screaming and jumping around, and all wearing those frilly dresses that Liz wants and Mom won't buy. Every girl had long hair and a big bow stuck to the back of her head. It looked like a flock of giant butterflies had landed and was trying to carry everybody away. I took a quick count. Five! And these were just the ones who'd come early.

Mrs. Norton was hanging onto Amanda and me like she thought we were going to make a break for it. Mrs. Norton, I decided, was not stupid. "The theme of this birthday is a tea party," she said in a loud voice.

Amanda nodded like this made sense and tugged at her skirt.

"Before they have tea, the girls are going to get dressed up." Mrs. Norton pulled us farther down the hall. A big glittery sign was taped to a closed door. The sign said, "Darling Dress Boutique." Mrs. Norton looked at Amanda. "I thought you could work in here."

She opened the door. The bed was covered with the fancy kind of nightgowns that women wear in movies and TV shows. High-heeled shoes were scattered around on the floor. Mrs. Norton gave a funny little laugh. "Tiffany loves negligees and high-heeled shoes." Amanda and I looked at each other, but neither one of us said anything. "Amanda, you can help the girls pick out an outfit and get dressed."

Amanda walked into the room and looked around. "Okay," she said and tugged at her skirt again.

Mrs. Norton led me farther down the hall.

We passed another door with another glittery sign. This one said, "Beautiful Beauty Salon." Mrs. Norton waved her free hand. "I'll be in there, and you . . . you, Jonah . . ." She smiled at me in a way I wasn't sure I liked. "You can be our cosmetologist."

I heaved a big sigh of relief. I was just going to ask her what a Russian astronaut was doing at a tea party when we came to the next door. The sign said, "Marvelous Makeup." Mrs. Norton flung open the door.

It was a bathroom. "I thought this would be best," Mrs. Norton said, "in case of spills. Over here," and she waved her hand at the counter under the mirror, "is mascara and lipstick and eye shadow. The girls can probably do that themselves." I nodded. I definitely thought that, too. "But over here," and her hand waved again, in the general direction of the toilet and the counter next to it, "over here, well, I thought you could sit and do face painting. You know, hearts, flowers, moons. Like at the fair?"

Just wait, I thought, until I got my hands on Amanda Matzinger.

There was a crash in the living room. "Oh, no!" Mrs. Norton ran out of the room.

I closed the lid, sat down on the john and looked at the face paints. They were in little open jars, and they kind of looked like pudding. Really noxious-looking pudding. I stuck my finger in one, and a bright glob of yellow stuck to my fingertip. I wiped it on my pants leg.

Mrs. Norton poked her head into the room. "I almost forgot. Try not to get any of that on their clothes. It stains." She disappeared again.

Amanda poked her head in.

"Come here," I said. I crooked my yellow-stained finger at her. "Come closer."

"She said *games.* I swear, Jonah, she said we were going to be running the games."

I picked up one of the little jars. "Do you know what this is, Amanda?"

"Makeup or something?"

I shook my head. "It's paint, Amanda." I waved the jar at her. "You promised no paint!"

She shrugged. "I gotta get back to the store." And she disappeared, too.

I sat there, staring at the yellow stripe on my new jeans. Nothing was worth this. Not even a trip to the beach.

The door opened again. "If you blab this—" I started.

A little girl was standing in the doorway. I mean, a really little girl.

"I need to go potty," she said.

I got out of there fast and stood out in the hall. I figured Mrs. Norton would be guarding the front door, but maybe there was a back way out.

Before I could move, Mrs. Norton came running down the hall. "What are you doing out of your station? We're ready to start!"

The toilet flushed, and the door opened. "Oh," Mrs. Norton said. "You were supposed to use the other bathroom, Ashley." She knelt down and started fussing with the little kid's frilly dress. Then she smiled up at me. "This is Ashley. She's the birthday girl's sister. Why don't you start with her, Jonah?"

Mrs. Norton propelled Ashley back into the bathroom and sat her down on a little stool in front of the toilet. I sat down again. "She'd love to have her face painted. Wouldn't you, sweetheart?" Mrs. Norton left without waiting for an answer.

Ashley looked at me like I had fangs.

"So," I said, "you like face painting?"

She burst into tears. "I like finger painting," she sobbed. "I don't want to paint with my face."

"No, no." I waved my hands around. "Look . . . see . . . you don't paint *with* your face. You paint your face. I mean, I paint your face. Like this." I stuck a Q-Tip into a jar and smudged a blob of red on my cheek. "See? It's a flower. Neat, huh?"

Ashley leaned forward. She sniffed a couple of times. "That's not a flower."

I looked in the mirror. She was right. It was a blob. "That was just practice. I'll do better on you. What do you want? A flower? A heart?"

She stuck her thumb in her mouth and mumbled something that sounded like "heart." The face paints were sort of gooey, but I got the hang of it and managed to get a big red heart on her cheek. She looked in the mirror and said, "I'll show Mommy." I couldn't tell if she was going to show Mommy because she was happy or mad.

I wiped the sweat off my forehead and heaved a sigh. The next two kids were real seven-year-olds. They both had on high heels, about four scarves wrapped around their necks, and lacy nightgowns over their dresses. I wondered if Mrs. Norton had gotten all this stuff out of her own closet.

Both kids wanted hearts and rainbows. By the time I was done, I'd gotten pretty good with face paints, and I'd decided murder was too good for Amanda.

My next customer plopped down in front of me. She was wearing a polka-dot nightgown that covered her from her neck to her feet. Her hair was sticking out, and it smelled so strongly of mousse it made my eyes water.

"I want a unicorn," she said. "A white unicorn."

I groaned. "Kid, who do you think I am? Rembrandt?"

She laughed. "I know who you are. You're Liz Truman's big brother."

"Yeah," I said, "and I can't draw unicorns. How about a Porsche?"

"What color?"

"Red. I do a *great* red Porsche."

She looked at the pots of paints. "Pink," she said. "I want a pink Porsche, like Barbie's."

I shrugged. "No problem."

The door opened, and Mr. Norton came into the bathroom. He was balancing a honking huge video camera on his shoulder. "Don't mind me," he said. "Just act like I'm not here."

The kid started to giggle, and I had to redo the front end of the car.

Mr. Norton pulled his head away from the eyepiece. "What is that you're drawing?"

I felt my face getting red. Maybe sports cars weren't exactly what they'd had in mind. "It's supposed to be a Porsche," I said.

Mr. Norton nodded. "I thought so." He went back to recording.

I lost count of all the faces I painted. Every time the door would open, I'd hear bursts of noise and laughter. I wondered if they were busing kids into this party.

After about four days, Amanda came back in. Her face was red, and her bangs were sticking up, and her skirt was twisted around kind of funny. She slumped against the counter. "Mrs. Norton said they're doing cake now. Boy, am I exhausted."

"You are! I have permanent face-painter's cramp."

She laughed, like this was really funny. "Come on," she said. "Mrs. Norton said we could have some cake."

We followed the party noises into the dining room. Mrs. Norton came over. "You did great," she said. "It wouldn't have gone nearly so well without you." She looked at the kids sitting around the table. "All we have now is opening the presents and watching the video, and Earl and I can handle that." She handed Amanda an envelope. "You did such a good job, I paid you extra. There's cake in the kitchen if you want to take a piece home with you."

"Thanks," Amanda said. "Feel free to tell your friends about our service."

"Service?" I said, when we were alone in the kitchen. "What service?"

Amanda cut a piece of cake and handed it to me. "A & J, Inc. Birthday Backup. I thought of it while I was helping dress kids. We'll make a fortune."

I shook my head. "Not me. You couldn't pay me to do this again."

She poked me and left frosting on my shirt. "Come on. Admit it. It wasn't that bad."

"Ha!" I said. I wiped at the frosting and watched her rip open the envelope.

Her eyes got big and she pulled out a handful of bills. "Twenty dollars, Jonah." She waved the money at me. "When have you ever been paid ten bucks for an hour's work?"

"An hour? It seemed a lot longer than that." I took my money and stuffed it into my pocket. Maybe Amanda was right. Maybe it hadn't been that bad. I bit a big pink rose off my piece of cake. "I could probably do it again," I mumbled. I swallowed the gob of frosting. "After all, they can't possibly get any worse than this, can they?"

CHAPTER FOUR

Jonah Likes Katherine

I spent most of Monday and Tuesday at school trying to avoid Mr. Decker. If I spotted him coming out of his office or standing in the hallway, I went the other way. I was late for social studies because he was talking to some kid across the hall and I couldn't get past them to the classroom.

On Wednesday, Amanda stopped by my desk in language arts. "Guess what?" she said.

"What?"

"Mrs. Norton was so impressed, she told her sister all about us. We may have another job this weekend."

I started figuring in my head. If we made ten bucks a party, and if we did a party every weekend, we could rent a limo and drive to Astoria.

"By the way, whose car was that in your driveway last night?"

I stopped figuring. "What car?"

"My dad and I were walking Skipper, and there was a car in your driveway."

"It was a repair man. He was . . . repairing."

"Funny. I thought I'd seen that car before."

Amanda shrugged. "Keep Saturday open, anyway, okay?"

"Okay."

She stopped by Kevin's desk. Kevin said something I couldn't hear, and Amanda laughed like it was really funny. I wondered if they were talking about me. Amanda sat down in front of Shawna.

Travis Hunter slid into the seat in front of me. He leaned back and whispered, "Keeping Saturday open for Moose Matzinger, huh, Jonah?"

I made a face. "Oh, yeah. Right," I said, and I laughed, although I was glad that Amanda was too far away to hear.

"She's way too tall for you, Jonah," Travis said. "Guy like you wants to concentrate on somebody his own size. Like Melissa. Or Katherine Chang." He waggled his eyebrows up and down and laughed.

"Okay. Thanks for the advice, Travis." I opened my notebook and tried to look busy.

He leaned closer, but his voice got louder. "What's the matter? I thought you liked Katherine."

Jerry Fitzner sat down across the aisle. "Jonah likes Katherine?" he said. He tapped Kevin on the shoulder. "Did you know Jonah's going out with Katherine?"

Kevin turned around and looked at me. "You didn't tell me that."

"I'm not going out with Katherine!" I said.

The room got really, really quiet. Everybody was looking at me. Over by the window, I saw Katherine look back at me once, real quick. Her long black hair swung against her face, but I could see she was blushing, too. Shawna said something to Amanda, and Amanda frowned.

Mr. Hickox came in then and started talking about how to write a persuasive paragraph. I slumped back in my desk. I wished the earthquake warning bell would ring, and all the floors and walls would start wobbling and crumbling. I imagined kids jumping up and screaming, trying to squeeze under their desks, and Katherine knocked down and pinned under a falling piece of roof. I fought my way to her side and lifted the beam and picked her up. . . .

In front of me, Travis stuck his foot out into the aisle. Janet Mendez was sitting across from him. She slid her foot out and stomped on Travis's. They both laughed. Travis pulled his foot loose and tried to step on Janet's, only she jerked it back too fast. She stuck her tongue out at him. She slid her foot out again, and this time Travis got it.

I tried to imagine that the school was on fire, and that Katherine was trapped in the gym, only I couldn't stop watching Travis and Janet and their feet. It was really depressing. Never in a million years could I do that with Katherine. And she probably hated me so much now, she'd just break my foot.

Kevin and I ate lunch together. He spent most of the period telling me about this movie he'd rented called *Thanksgiving Hatchet Massacre II.* Hot lunch was turkey and mashed potatoes with gravy, so it all fit in.

We carried our trays up to the window. "Health next," Kevin said. He made it sound much worse than a Thanksgiving massacre.

"Changes in our bodies," I said. I dumped my silverware into the tub of soapy water.

"It's the same stuff they taught us last year," Kevin said. "It's a waste of time. I'd rather do fitness."

"At least we don't have to change our clothes for health."

Kevin shook his head. "It's still a waste. They never tell you anything you need to know."

That was true. Just once, I wished somebody would tell us how you actually talked to a girl. I mean, you'd think you'd need to know how to do that before you'd need any of the technical stuff. "You're right," I said. "It's a waste."

We went out the cafeteria doors, and Mr. Decker was standing right there, talking to Ms. Perkins. I stopped so fast, my feet skidded and squeaked on the linoleum. I grabbed Kevin and dragged him down the hall and around the corner.

"I thought he liked Miss McNeal," Kevin said.

"Shut up," I said.

Travis and Jerry and Brad Smith were standing outside the door of the health classroom. Travis was holding something and Jerry and Brad were looking at it. All three of them were laughing.

"Oh, great," Kevin muttered.

Brad saw us and waved a hand. "Hey, you guys. Come look."

Travis had a copy of *Penthouse* magazine. He had it open to the centerfold, and he was looking it over. "Not bad," he said finally.

"Where'd you get that?" I said. I glanced back over my shoulder. A bunch of sixth graders were standing around, waiting to get into a class.

"Not in the school library," Jerry said, and they all laughed again.

"It's my dad's," Brad said. "I borrowed it from his stash under the bed."

Travis had turned the page. "Now this," he said, "is what I call health. Adamson should show us this, instead of those stupid diagrams." He turned the magazine so we all could see.

"You can see the same thing on cable TV," Kevin said. "And it moves."

"Oh, right, Martinez," Jerry said. "I'm sure your parents let you watch that stuff."

I looked back again, trying to see if the sixth graders were still there. They were gone. Katherine Chang was coming down the hall instead, with Lisa Tate and Chelsea from my algebra class. They saw us and headed in our direction.

The turkey and mashed potatoes sank farther into my stomach, and I wished I'd skipped lunch. Katherine looked really serious. Lisa nodded toward me and said something, and Katherine frowned.

I moved, trying to get into the classroom, but Travis was standing between me and the door. He was looking at Katherine over my head. He was smiling.

I turned around, and Katherine walked right up to me. "Hi, Jonah," she said. And she smiled.

All of the air was suddenly sucked right out of the hallway. Maybe right out of the entire school. I couldn't get a breath in or out. Part of my brain said, "Hi, Katherine," loud and clear, but the connection to my mouth seemed to be broken. The rest of my brain started shrieking, "Help! Help! We aren't getting any oxygen in here!"

"Nice sweater, Katherine," Travis said. He nudged Brad. "Isn't that a nice sweater Katherine's got on?"

Katherine's face got red. Lisa and Chelsea both moved closer, and Lisa made a gagging sound.

Travis and Jerry laughed. I hated it when Travis said stuff like that. I hated it when he laughed that stupid laugh. The air rushed back into my lungs. "It's not a nice sweater!" I said.

Everybody looked at me. Travis raised his eyebrows. "It's not a nice sweater, Jonah?"

"No! I mean . . . well . . . yes, it is nice . . . but . . ." What I wanted to say was that we all knew Travis was being a jerk, but now I was being a jerk myself.

"I can't believe it. That's disgusting." Chelsea was pointing at the *Penthouse* dangling open from Travis's hand.

Katherine and Lisa rolled their eyes. "Don't you know that that's exploitation of women?" Lisa said.

Travis looked at the magazine. He looked at Katherine. "Gee," he said, "I just know it's fun to look at. Don't you think it's fun to look at, Jonah?"

I turned around and stared at the locker behind me. It was an orange locker, a very nice orange locker. I wondered who owned this locker. I wondered if I would fit inside it.

"You stink, Travis Hunter," Lisa said. I could hear all three of them moving off down the hall.

Travis laughed again. He put his hand on my shoulder, and I turned around, slowly.

"Really lame, Truman," Travis said. He shook his head and looked sad. "A girl talks to you, you need to say something back. Standing there, turning blue, that's not cool." He held out the *Penthouse.* "Here. You need this more than I do."

He gave it a toss. The magazine slapped onto the floor between us.

Mr. Decker walked around the corner.

None of us moved. We all just stood there, watching him come toward us. Nobody looked at the magazine, lying face up on the floor.

Brad and Jerry both moved, simultaneously. "Gotta go," Brad said. "Don't want to be late," Jerry said. They went into the classroom.

Mr. Decker focused on us, and his face got that "Where are you boys supposed to be?" look.

Travis bent down and picked up the magazine. "Here, Jonah," he said. "I think you dropped this."

Kevin made a funny little gurgling noise.

I grabbed the magazine and slipped it inside my notebook, just as Mr. Decker came up to us. He looked from Travis to me to Kevin and back to Travis. I gripped the notebook tighter. "Where are you boys supposed to be?"

"Health," Travis said. He gave Mr. Decker a big smile. "Human development. In fact, we were just discussing the topic out here."

Mr. Decker frowned. "Well, I think you'd learn more inside the classroom, Travis, with Mr. Adamson."

We all nodded. Mr. Decker reached out and opened the classroom door. He looked right at me. I gripped my notebook tighter and waited for him to say something, something about the magazine or something about my mother. I wasn't sure which would be worse.

But he didn't say anything at all. He just stood there, holding the door open.

We filed into the classroom. I could feel him watching me all the way to my desk.

CHAPTER FIVE

Worse Than Halloween

I couldn't figure out how to get the *Penthouse* back to Brad, so I ended up taking it home with me and shoving it into the bottom drawer of my desk, under the model rocket I'd never finished building. I spent the rest of the week waiting for Mr. Decker to call me into his office, but he never did. Maybe he hadn't even seen the stupid magazine. Or maybe he was just torturing me.

On Saturday afternoon, Amanda and I worked for Mrs. Norton's sister. The party was at Piccolo Pizza Pandemonium. Amanda and I each got five seven-year-olds and pockets full of tokens. I got into the high scores twice in Star Stomper, and Amanda won so many tickets playing Skeeball that we divided them all up among the kids. I lost one little boy in the Ball Crawl, but he showed up in the Pizza Pandemonium Theater before anybody else noticed. Mrs. Norton's sister only paid us five bucks apiece, but I didn't mind. I couldn't wait for Dad to call so I could tell him that somebody *had* paid me to play video games.

I got home around five o'clock. "I'm home!" I shouted as I slammed the door.

"We're up here!" Mom shouted back.

I grabbed an apple from the kitchen and went up to her bedroom.

Liz was sitting in the middle of Mom's bed. There were dresses and skirts all around her. Mom was standing in front of the full-length mirror. She was wearing a red-and-white dress I'd never seen before.

"How did it go?" she asked.

"Great. I got into the high scores twice." I took a bite of the apple. "Is that a new dress?"

"No." She turned and looked at herself sideways. "Do you think it's too tight?"

The dress had a low neck, and it was kind of tight. I thought it looked weird. Mom usually wears jeans and T-shirts. "It's fine," I said and took another bite of apple.

"I liked the blue one better," Liz said. She held up the edge of a dress lying next to her.

Mom sighed. She ran her hands down the sides of the dress and turned the other way.

"You're going out with Mr. Decker again?" I said. "Don't you think you're seeing an awful lot of him?" I took another bite of the apple, and juice ran down my chin. I wiped at it with the back of my hand.

Mom looked at me in the mirror. "We enjoy each other's company, Jonah. It's really no—"

" 'Big deal,' " I said with her. "Where are you going this time?"

"To a concert and dinner." She was looking at herself again. "Maybe the blue one is better."

"I think Bob's nice," Liz said.

"Bob?" I nearly choked on the apple piece. "You call Mr. Decker Bob?"

"He said I could." Liz rubbed a piece of a dress against her cheek. "When you were hiding upstairs."

"I was cleaning the hamster cage," I said. "Winifred and Dorothy like a clean cage."

"Oh, yeah. Right."

"And I had to practice."

Liz rolled her eyes.

The doorbell rang.

They both looked at me.

"I'm really not quite ready," Mom said.

Liz sighed. "I'll get it. I'm not scared."

"I'll get it," I said.

I turned and headed down the stairs. If he asked me about the *Penthouse*, I'd say that I'd picked it up because I didn't want some sixth grader to find it. I'd tell him that I'd only been trying to protect the younger kids. I crossed the hall and opened the door.

It was like opening the door on Halloween night, only worse. Mr. Decker was standing there on our front porch. In the flesh. And in the ugly tie. He was carrying two bunches of flowers.

"Hi," he said.

"Hi," I said. I cleared my throat, getting ready with the story.

He cleared *his* throat. "Is your mom here?"

"Oh. Yeah." I backed up a little. "Come on in."

He stepped into the front hall, and I shut the door. He put both bunches of flowers into his left hand and stuck out his right hand. "It's good to finally meet you at home."

I couldn't tell if that was some kind of snide remark. He was smiling, though, and his hand was hanging there in midair. I realized that I was still holding the apple core. I set it on the table by the door and wiped my hand on my pants leg. I took his hand, and stared hard at the tie. It had dinosaurs on it. I pulled my hand loose.

He nodded toward the bunches of flowers. "I got these for your mother and—"

"Hi, Bob!" Liz came galloping down the stairs.

Mr. Decker held out the smaller bunch of flowers. "For Liz," he said, and he made this funny little bow.

"For me?" Liz squealed. She looked around the room, like maybe there were twenty or thirty other people who were supposed to get flowers. Then she grabbed the bouquet and squished it against her. "Thank you, thank you, thank you," she said, and she started twirling around and around.

I thought I was going to barf.

Mom came down the stairs. She was wearing the blue dress. It had a big, swirly kind of skirt. She looked like the woman in that old TV show they rerun on Saturday afternoons. "Oh, my goodness," she said. She stood on the bottom step, smiling, and watching Liz twirl.

Mr. Decker held out the other bouquet, without bowing or saying anything.

Mom took the flowers. She bent her head down to smell them, and when she looked up again, I thought how pretty she looked, in that dress, with the flowers and all.

"Thank you, Bob," she said. "It was really sweet of you."

Sweet. Not only was he cute, Mr. Decker was sweet, too.

"Just let me put them in some water." Mom went off to the kitchen, with Liz twirling after her.

Mr. Decker looked at me. He shuffled his feet back and forth. "I'm sorry I didn't bring anything for you, Jonah. I was just passing the florist's and I thought . . . well . . ."

"That's okay." I stepped onto the stair behind

me. Then I went up another one. I could almost look him in the eye. "It was nice," I said.

He nodded and smiled, and his feet shuffled on the carpet again. I wondered how much static electricity he was building up.

Mom came back with the flowers in a vase. "Aren't they gorgeous?" she said to nobody in particular.

"I like mine better," Liz said. Hers had fit into one of Mom's "Best Teacher in the World" coffee cups.

Mom put her flowers on the coffee table in the living room. I noticed I'd left a cereal bowl there that morning. I thought she was going to say something, but she didn't.

"I'm going to put mine in my room," Liz said. She gave Mr. Decker this big, goofy smile, and he smiled back at her.

"We're going to dinner and then to a concert," Mom said to me.

"I know," I said.

"There's leftover lasagne. You can heat it in the microwave. And I left a fruit salad in the fridge."

"I know," I said again, even though I hadn't known about the food.

"I left the phone numbers and our seat numbers on the pad by the phone."

"I know," I said, louder.

Mr. Decker put his hand on her elbow. "They'll be fine, Ellen. I'm sure Jonah is very responsible." He smiled at me.

I didn't smile back.

"Well," Mom said, "we won't be late." She bent down and kissed Liz. "Be good," she said.

Mr. Decker opened the door and sort of ushered Mom out with his other arm. I watched to see if he kept his arm around her, but the door closed before I could tell. I didn't know if I'd really wanted to know.

Liz ran over to the window and watched them go. "Bye!" she shouted. She waved her hand back and forth like it was on fire or something. "Bye, Bob!"

I pulled her back and shut the curtain. "Why do you act like a two-year-old around him?"

She frowned. "I wasn't acting like a two-year-old."

"Yes, you were."

"No, I wasn't."

"Yes—" I stopped. "Never mind," I said. I twitched the curtain aside and watched the car drive off down the street. I wondered what Mom and Mr. Decker talked about when they were alone.

The phone rang. "I'll get it." I ran upstairs and grabbed it in Mom's room.

"Hi. It's Kevin."

"Hi." I pushed a couple of dresses aside and sat down on the edge of the bed.

"What are you doing?"

"Nothing. What are you doing?"

"I got a new graphics program. I've been reading the manual."

"Oh." Kevin is the only person I know who actually reads those things.

"I'm going to install the program tonight. You want to come over?"

"I can't, Kev. I have to baby-sit Liz."

"Oh." There was silence, then Kevin said, "You know what just happened?"

"What?"

"Laurie Peters called and asked if I wanted to go out with her." Kevin laughed.

I didn't know who Laurie Peters was, but I felt a little stab of jealousy. Maybe a big stab. The only girl who ever called me was Amanda, with her dumb business ideas. "What did you say?"

"I said I'd think about it."

I leaned back on the headboard and looked at myself in the mirror. "Which one is Laurie Peters?"

"She's that one in band. You know. The blonde who plays the trumpet."

I shook my head. "No. That's Chris Meyer. I know because I had to help her sort music one time."

"Oh." Kevin was quiet again for a second. "Are you sure? I thought the blonde was Laurie Peters."

"Nope. Chris Meyer is definitely the blonde on trumpet."

"No kidding. So who do you think Laurie Peters is?"

I laughed. "I bet she wears glasses. And she's fat. I bet she's a sixth grader. I bet you're going to be going out with a fat sixth grader, Kevin."

"I didn't say I was going to go out with her. I said I'd think about it. Jeez. You're sure she's not in band?"

"I'm sure."

"Oh, well. See you Monday, okay?"

"Okay."

I hung up. Then I picked the phone back up. "Hi, Katherine?" I said to the dial tone. "Katherine. I really like you a lot. And I was wondering if you'd like to go out with me?" The tone buzzed. "You would? Great!"

I looked up. Liz was standing in the doorway. I slammed the phone down. "Get lost!" I shouted.

"Jonah's got a girlfriend!" She ran down the hall, cackling.

I leaned back against the headboard. "I wish," I said, to my reflection. "I just wish you did."

CHAPTER SIX

Going Out

Amanda stopped me as we were coming out of the band room Monday afternoon. "Mrs. Norton's sister told her neighbor, and we have another job this Saturday. Word's really getting around."

"Yeah," I said. Before we started this party business, Amanda almost never talked to me at school. Now it seemed like we were talking all the time. I checked up and down the hall, to make sure Travis wasn't around. "Is this another tea party or is it going to be a fun one?"

Amanda frowned. "Jonah. It doesn't sound very professional to ask customers if the party is going to be fun."

"Well, did you at least say no paint?"

She patted me on the arm. "Jonah. As president of A & J, Inc., I have only your best interests at heart."

I moved my arm out of her reach. "President? Who made you president?"

"I did."

"Oh, so what am I?"

She grinned. "You're everybody else."

"Hey, Jonah." Jerry Fitzner came out of the band room with Kelsey Waters. "I think you dropped this."

He held up my spit rag. Actually, it was an old diaper my mom had given me to replace the original spit rag that I'd lost. I grabbed it and stuffed it into my pocket. Jerry and Kelsey laughed.

Amanda looked at the rag hanging out of my pocket. "I can't believe you just did that. That thing's disgusting."

"What was I supposed to do?"

Amanda shrugged. "I would have said it wasn't mine."

"Everybody in the brass section knows it's mine." I watched Jerry put his arm around Kelsey and say something. Kelsey laughed again. "I'd give anything to be able to do that," I said.

Amanda glanced back over her shoulder. "What? Walk and tell dirty jokes at the same time?"

"No. Talk to girls like that. When I'm around a girl, I can't even get my mouth to open."

Amanda looked at me. She blinked her eyes a couple of times. Then she punched me in the arm.

"Hey!" I said. "Why'd you do that?"

"Aren't I a girl?"

"Of course you're a girl, but . . . You're different."

"Who's different?" Kevin had come out of the band room.

"Never mind." Amanda smiled at Kevin. "Your solo sounded really great."

"Except he started a measure too soon," I said and laughed.

Kevin shook his head. "I'm having trouble concentrating today."

"But it sounded great. I mean, once you were in there." Amanda shoved her hair back over her shoulder and smiled some more.

"Hey," Kevin said, "do you know a girl named Laurie Peters?"

Amanda shook her head. "I don't think so." She frowned. "Why?"

"I was just wondering," Kevin said. "It's not important."

I laughed, and he punched me in the arm.

"Hey," I said, "why's everybody hitting me today?"

"Because you deserve it," Amanda said, and she stalked off down the hall.

"She looks mad," Kevin said. "What's she mad about?"

I shrugged. "I don't know. I didn't do anything."

We started walking toward science. "Still haven't figured out who Laurie Peters is, huh?" I said.

"No." He made a face. "I've spent the whole day trying to read people's names on their notebooks. Mrs. Fujino yelled at me in social studies because she thought I was cheating on a test."

I was keeping an eye out for Mr. Decker. I hadn't seen him all day. "Maybe you could get them to call her into the office. Then you could hang out and see who shows up."

"Oh, yeah. Great idea." Kevin snorted and I laughed.

"I even checked the yearbooks in the library," he said. "She isn't in any of them."

"Ha," I said. "She probably is a sixth grader."

"Or new," he said. "She could be new."

A group of eighth-grade girls walked past us. I waited until they were gone, then I said, "If you did find out who she was, and if it turned out you liked her, what would you do?"

Kevin shrugged. "I don't know."

"Would you go out with her?"

He shrugged again. "I guess."

"Where? I mean, if you were going to go out, where would you go?"

"I don't know. We'd just go out. When Brad was going out with Megan, they didn't go anywhere. They were just going out." He gave me a funny look. "Why are you asking all these dumb questions?"

I shrugged. "I was just wondering." It was another one of those things they never bothered to teach us in health.

We stopped in front of the science lab. "At least I don't really have to worry about it," I said. "Laurie Peters didn't call me."

He made a barfing noise. Then he said, "Can you spend the night Friday night?"

"I don't know. I'll have to check. I may have to baby-sit again."

"How come you have to baby-sit all the time lately?"

I took a deep breath. "Mom's busy lately."

"Well, I've got that new program running. It's really cool. And I'm going to rent *Thanksgiving Hatchet Massacre III.*"

"Okay," I said. "I'll call you tonight."

I thought about Kevin and Laurie Peters through most of science. I wondered if girls would call me if my hair was dark and curly, instead of straight and boring and brown. I imagined getting one of those permanents and a pair of dark brown contact lenses. I imagined girls calling me up, leaving messages on our answering machine. I imagined Katherine Chang coming over to my desk in language arts. When Mr. Jacobi called on me, I jumped and said, "What?" in a really loud voice. Everybody laughed.

When I got home, Mom and Liz were already in the living room. Liz was practicing the piano, and Mom was sitting on the couch listening to her, although it looked like she was asleep. She opened her eyes when I came in. "Hi there. How was school?"

"Fine."

Liz looked up from the keyboard. "Did you see Bob? Did you say hi to Bob?"

"No." I put my horn on the floor and dropped my books on the coffee table. "I don't see Mr. Decker every day."

"Too bad. This is called 'Little Dancing Fireflies.' "

Mom sat up and rubbed her eyes. "That sounds great, honey." I raised my eyebrows at her, and she smiled.

"Kevin wants to know if I can spend the night Friday," I said.

Mom frowned. "This Friday?"

"Yeah."

"This is called 'Happy, Smiling Flowers,' " Liz said. It sounded exactly like the firefly thing to me, but I didn't say anything. I was watching Mom. I didn't like the way she was looking at her shoes under the coffee table instead of at me.

"You know," she said, "there was something I wanted to talk to you guys about."

I hate it when adults say that. I just hate it. Liz stopped right in the middle of the happy flowers.

Mom cleared her throat. "Bob's daughter has

asked us over for dinner. Us and Bob, of course."

I blew my breath out in a loud puff. I wasn't sure what I'd been expecting her to say, but that wasn't it.

"Bob has a daughter?" Liz was looking at Mom over her shoulder. "I thought you said he wasn't married."

"Well, he was married," Mom said. "His wife died. About ten years ago."

"Oh, that's sad." Liz puckered her face up. "Bob must be sad."

"Yes. Well. He's better now," Mom said. "Diane, Bob's daughter, wants us all to come over and meet her husband and her kids." Mom looked at me.

"So I can't go to Kevin's."

"Not this Friday," Mom said. "Maybe next week."

Liz turned around completely on the piano bench. "Bob's daughter has kids?" She sounded like Bob's daughter had two heads.

"Little ones, I think," Mom said. "Two boys. One's four and the other's just a little over a year."

"Oh, boy," Liz said. "I like babies."

"I'm hungry," I said.

I went into the kitchen and got a handful of cookies and sat down at the table.

Liz and Mom followed me. "I'm hungry,

too," Liz said. She climbed up onto the counter to get down the cereal. Mom went over and opened the refrigerator. "Gee," she said, "what do you guys feel like having for dinner?"

I didn't say anything. I didn't even feel much like eating the cookies. Thinking about dinner with Mr. Decker had made me lose my appetite.

Liz poured the cereal into a cup. "Can I eat this in the living room?"

Mom frowned. Then she nodded. "Okay. But don't spill."

"Why do I have to go to this dinner, anyway?" I said when Liz was gone.

Mom shut the refrigerator door and came and sat down at the table. "We're all invited, Jonah. I want us all to go."

I started picking the chocolate chips out of one of the cookies. "If this is no big deal, like you keep saying, why do we have to meet his daughter and his grandkids and everybody?"

"I think she wants to meet me, actually." Mom swept cookie crumbs up into a little pile. "I think she's checking me out."

"So you don't need me there."

"But I'd like you to be there." Mom put her hand on my hand. "I need the moral support, Jonah. I'm not really prepared for all this dating stuff." She shook her head. "It's certainly not what I thought I'd be doing at my age."

"Or his age," I said.

She smiled. "He looks older than he really is, you know."

"That's what Amanda said."

"You and Amanda talk about Bob?" She looked surprised.

"Not about you and him. Just him in general. You know, he is the principal," I added.

"Well, this is simply a little family get-together. Bob and I are just going out."

I groaned. I'd already gone through this with Kevin. I'd heard enough about going out to last me for a long time.

Liz came back in the kitchen. She still had the cup of cereal in her hand, and she had a funny look on her face. "I just thought of something," she said. "If you marry Bob, you'll be a *grandmother.*"

"Oh, honey," Mom said. She gave a funny little laugh. She looked at me and then back at Liz. "That's a long way down the road."

I didn't know what that was supposed to mean. I stood up so fast my chair banged against the counter. "I have to practice," I said, and I went upstairs.

CHAPTER SEVEN

Mallory

Mr. Decker's daughter lived in one of the new developments they're building all over the place.

"Wow," Liz said as we pulled up in front of the house on Friday night, "just like in a TV show."

"The garage is bigger than our entire house," I said.

Mom leaned forward and peered out the windshield. "Remember, everybody's on their best behavior."

I looked back at Liz. "That means no picking your nose at the table." Liz giggled. Mom ignored me.

As we climbed out of the car, she said, "Tuck in your shirt, Jonah."

"Mom. It looks stupid when I tuck in my shirt. Do you want them to think we're stupid?"

Her face had those little lines it gets on parent conference nights. She started up the big front steps. "I just want them to think we're people who tuck in their shirts."

I tucked in my shirt. Mom straightened the

bow on Liz's jumper and smoothed her own hair. She looked at both of us and smiled. Then she rang the doorbell.

A little boy with curly blond hair and big blue eyes opened the door. He was wearing green-and-white striped overalls. He looked at us without saying anything.

"Well," Mom said, "hello there."

The kid shut the door.

Liz laughed. Mom rang the doorbell again. Nothing happened. I started to laugh, too. Mom rang the bell again.

A woman opened the door this time. She had curly hair, too, but it was dark. I figured this was probably Mr. Decker's daughter, Diane, even though she didn't have a big nose. She had another little kid riding on her hip. He looked exactly like the first kid, even down to the overalls, but smaller. "Oh my goodness," Diane said. "I told Tucker to answer the door. I'm so sorry. Come in. Come in."

The inside of the house looked kind of like the outside—clean and new and like nobody really lived there. You could see the vacuum-cleaner tracks on the rug in the living room.

Diane shifted the kid to her other hip. "It's so nice to finally meet you, Ellen," she said. "Dad's told us so much about you."

Mom blushed, which is something I don't

often see her do. "Thank you for having us over, Diane. What a lovely house."

A tall man came out of the kitchen. His hair was blond, too, and what there was of it was all slicked straight back from his forehead. "This is my husband, Brian," Diane said. "And you met Tucker, I guess." She jiggled the kid in her arms. "This is Cooper."

Cooper put his face in her neck.

Mom introduced Liz and me. Diane sort of nodded and smiled, but Brian came over and shook my hand. His hand felt warm and damp. "I've been slaving in the kitchen," he said, and he and Diane and Mom all laughed.

"Dad should be here any minute," Diane said. "Let's sit in the living room, Ellen." She looked over her shoulder. "Tucker! Tucker, come here!"

Tucker poked his head around a corner.

"Sweetie, come be a big boy and show Liz and Jonah where the playroom is."

Great. I'd given up *Thanksgiving Hatchet Massacre III* to spend the evening in a playroom with a four-year-old and my little sister.

Tucker led us up a wide staircase. Liz ran her hand along the shiny wooden banister. "I bet this would be great to slide down."

Tucker looked at her. "You'd fall and crack your head wide open, and there'd be blood all over."

Liz widened her eyes, and I laughed. This kid should be watching movies with Kevin.

The playroom was huge. The walls were covered with shelves full of little-kid toys: castles and barns and lots of plastic figures. A wooden rocking horse with a black bristly tail took up most of one corner. A couch was facing a big TV with a VCR and a Nintendo. The TV was on; it looked like somebody had been watching MTV.

"You can't play with anything," Tucker said.

"Tucker." A girl sat up on the couch. She looked about my age. She had long blonde hair and those same big blue eyes. She smiled. She had a great smile. "Hi," she said.

I put my hands on my hips. Then I crossed my arms instead. "Hi," I said, and my voice did that high-pitched thing it does. I cleared my throat, but I was afraid to try again.

"You're not supposed to watch that channel when I'm in the room," Tucker said.

The girl rolled her eyes at me. She clicked off the TV, stood up, and came around the couch.

My heart did a double beat. She was shorter than me. By a whole inch. Maybe two. "I'm Mallory," she said.

I cleared my throat again.

"I'm Liz," Liz said. She jerked her thumb in my direction. "This is Jonah."

I nodded. That was right. That was my name.

"She's my stepsister," Tucker said. "That means she has to sit on the steps." He shoved past her and turned the TV back on. He turned on the Nintendo and started playing.

Mallory ignored him. "You guys want something to drink? Diane put some stuff up here for us." She pointed to a table with some cans of pop and bowls of pretzels and chips.

All of a sudden, I remembered this huge zit that was forming on my chin. I wondered how big it had gotten during the ride over here. I imagined it being about the size of a Ping-Pong ball.

Mallory smiled. "Well? Coke? 7UP?"

"7UP," Liz said.

I put my hand over my chin, like I was thinking really hard about what I wanted. "Coke," I managed to croak out. I coughed. "I think I'll have a Coke."

Mallory smiled that great smile and poured the drinks into cups. Liz took hers and went over to sit beside Tucker.

Mallory took a chip and bit the edge off one corner. "So. Where do you go to school?"

I was having trouble drinking and keeping my hand on my chin. "Walt Morey," I said. I put my hand in my pocket. "Middle School," I added. I took my hand out of my pocket.

"I go to Eric Kimmel." She bit another tiny piece off the chip. "I'd go to Morey if I lived here, but I live with my mom and her husband."

I nodded. I took a sip of the Coke. The carbonation stung the back of my throat, and my eyes started to water.

"What grade are you in?" Mallory asked.

"Seventh," I said. That sounded right, so I said it again. "Seventh."

"Me, too." She smiled that smile again. "Don't you love it? I absolutely loathed last year. They treated us like such babies."

"Yeah," I said, although, at the moment, I couldn't remember last year. I could barely even remember ten minutes ago.

"Grandpa seems really happy since he started dating your mom. Diane mentioned it . . . oh, about eighty times."

It took me a second to figure out that Grandpa must be Mr. Decker. "Yeah," I said. "It's great." I was beginning to think it *was* great.

Mallory nibbled another piece off the chip. I wondered how long she could make one chip last. "He's not really my grandfather, of course. I call him that because Tucker and Cooper do. I think that kind of thing really helps meld a stepfamily together."

"Oh, yeah. Me, too," I said. If Mom married Mr. Decker, would I be related to Mallory? At least I'd see her again, when the families were melding. Maybe I'd even see her a whole lot. There'd have to be a lot more melding. I realized she'd asked me a question. "What?"

"I asked you if your dad has remarried."

"Oh, yeah. Well. He's married, but they live in Seattle, I think. I mean, they do live in Seattle." I took another sip of the Coke. I thought about eating a chip, but I didn't know if I could handle two things at once.

"I want something to drink," Tucker said. "In the can. I want the whole can."

Mallory rolled her eyes at me, and I rolled mine back. She leaned closer to me. I could smell her hair spray or perfume or something. I could see the little tiny cracks in her lipstick. "My mother says Diane spoils them rotten," she whispered.

"Oh," I said.

She went over and gave Tucker his drink. I finished mine in one gulp and followed her.

"Get the rutabaga," Mallory said. She was leaning over the back of the couch, watching Tucker play the video game. "The rutabagas are good."

I leaned over beside her. Our legs were just almost nearly touching. "Actually," I said, "if he gets the star instead and then jumps on the next kangaroo, he'll warp automatically to level seven."

Mallory looked at me. "No kidding! I didn't know that!"

"Well." I rubbed my hand on the back of the couch. "You've gotta play it a lot."

Liz looked at us over her shoulder. "Jonah is very good at video games."

"I can tell that," Mallory said. She smiled, and I smiled back. Her hair was straight and really, really long. It swayed when she moved, like hair in a shampoo commercial.

"Well, how's everybody up here?" Mr. Decker walked into the room. I jumped a little and moved over by the arm of the couch.

"Grandpa!" Tucker screamed. He dropped the controller and climbed over the back of the couch. Liz grabbed his can of pop just before it went over with him. Tucker ran to Mr. Decker, and Mr. Decker scooped him up and gave him a big hug.

Mr. Decker came over by the couch. "Hello, Mallory." He reached out and ruffled her hair. "Hello, Jonah."

I moved a few steps back so he couldn't reach my hair. "Hi." I started to say "Mr. Decker," but that sounded dumb. "How are you?" I said, instead.

"Fine, fine." He gave Tucker another hug and patted him on the back.

I glanced at Liz. She wasn't jumping and

twirling. She was just sort of sitting there, watching Mr. Decker and Tucker.

Mr. Decker came around the side of the couch. He slid Tucker onto the floor and held his hand. He held his other hand out to Liz. "I've been sent to escort you to dinner, Miss Truman," he said.

Liz stood up and took his free hand. He bent down and whispered something in her ear. Liz smiled and looked happier.

Tucker pulled at his shirt. "Tell me a secret, too, Grandpa."

Mr. Decker smiled at him. "I'll tell you all a secret. Dinner's ready."

Tucker frowned. "That's not a secret."

"But it's going to be good," Mr. Decker said. He led the two of them out of the room.

Mallory was smoothing her hair where Mr. Decker had messed it up. She made a face at me.

"He's the principal of my school," I said.

"I know," she said. "Poor you."

I laughed, and she laughed, too. Dinner was going to be great.

CHAPTER EIGHT

Under the Table

We followed Mr. Decker and Liz and Tucker down the stairs. "What is for dinner, anyway?" Mallory asked.

"Dead ants," Tucker said.

"Mmm," Mr. Decker said. "My favorite." And he and Liz laughed.

I was concentrating hard on getting down the stairs behind Mallory without tripping. I untucked my shirt as I walked.

The dining-room table was set with a white tablecloth, shiny silverware, and flowers with candles. Mom was already sitting down. Cooper was sitting in a high chair near one end of the table. Mr. Decker parked Tucker in a chair near the other end. He pulled out the chair next to it for Liz.

I saw Mom frown at my shirt, but then Mr. Decker said, "Jonah, you sit there between your mom and Cooper."

I slid into the chair. Cooper looked at me like he thought I should sit in some other room. Mallory sat down across from me and smiled.

Mom leaned over and whispered, "Don't forget to use your napkin."

I unfolded my napkin and put it in my lap. Mallory turned to say something to Liz, and I turned to Mom and whispered, "Stop embarrassing me."

Mr. Decker leaned over from Mom's other side. "Did you need something, Jonah?"

Yes. A new mother. "No thanks," I said.

Cooper threw his plastic cup on the floor. I bent down to pick it up. He reached over and grabbed a handful of my hair and pulled, really hard.

"Ow!" I jerked back upright and plunked his cup down on his tray.

Liz looked across the table at me and started giggling. Tucker was laughing, too. Mallory bit her lip, and I knew she was being too nice to laugh.

"What's so funny?" I asked Liz, and she laughed even harder.

Mom reached over and smoothed my hair. "Don't worry about it. It looks fine."

I wanted to feel the top of my head, but I knew they were all just waiting for me to do that. I gave Cooper a dirty look. He held out his hand. It was smeared with gel. Served him right.

I checked out the food on the table. There was a big bowl of salad and a couple of loaves of

French bread. Next to my plate, there was a little bowl filled with something yellow and oily. It reminded me of the valve oil I use on my horn.

"Here we are. Just for you, Dad." Diane was standing in the doorway of the kitchen. She stepped aside, and Brian came in. He was carrying a big, huge platter. It was covered with bright red lobsters.

"Oh, sweetheart," Mr. Decker said. "You shouldn't have."

No kidding, I thought.

Brian started around the table. "One of my clients gets these wholesale," he said. He put a lobster on each plate. They clicked and clanked as they landed on the china. They didn't sound like real food.

"Oh boy," Mallory said. She looked down at her plate full of legs and claws and antennas. "Don't you just love lobster?"

"Oh boy," I said.

"It looks delicious," Mom said.

I looked at the lobster on my plate. It looked back at me with its beady, black, little eyes. Its antennas stuck up above its head. Its claws were so big, they hung off the edges of the plate, and its skinny, jointy little legs splayed out on either side of its body. Little stiff hairs stuck out all over the legs and along the plates in its back. It looked just exactly like a big huge insect. Tucker had been right. We were having dead ants for dinner.

Diane was standing behind Liz. "Ellen," she said, "I want you to know that, as a rule, the kids eat just what Brian and I eat. But . . . well . . ." She laughed. "I just can't see wasting good lobster on them, so I made some macaroni and cheese."

She pointed her finger down at the top of Liz's head and raised her eyebrows.

"Oh," Mom said, "I'm sure Liz would love to try—"

"Macaroni and cheese," Liz said. "My favorite. Don't waste a lobster on me."

Diane started spooning big orange globs of macaroni and cheese on the little kids' plates. I looked at Cooper. I bet he'd much rather have a nice, shiny, red lobster.

Cooper eyed me with *his* beady eyes. He shook his head back and forth and tried to bong me with the cup.

Brian and Diane were surveying the table. "Have we forgotten anything?" Diane asked.

"It all looks wonderful," Mom said.

"Oh. I brought a special bottle of wine," Mr. Decker said. He turned to Mom. "I found that chardonnay we had the other night." They smiled at each other.

"You help Dad, Brian," Diane said. "I have to get the milk."

"Can't we just eat?" Mallory said.

"Why don't you give us a hand, Mal," Brian said. "You can carry the glasses."

Mallory groaned, but she followed Mr. Decker and Brian and Diane into the kitchen.

I leaned closer to Mom. "How do you eat these things, anyway?" I poked my lobster with my knife.

Mom shook her head. "I have no idea. I've never eaten a whole lobster." All of a sudden, she started to laugh. She didn't make a sound, but I could tell by the way her shoulders shook that she was laughing really hard.

"Have you been drinking?" I whispered.

Mom shook her head, and her eyes were filling up with tears. "Unfortunately, no." She picked up one of her lobster's claws and waved it at me. "Hi, cutie," she said in a squeaky voice.

Liz and Tucker both burst out laughing, too. Even Cooper laughed. "Mom," I said, "is this your best behavior?"

Mr. Decker came back in carrying an open bottle of wine. He looked around the table. "Well, you all look like you're enjoying yourselves."

Mom wiped her eyes with her napkin. "Oh, we are, Bob. We are."

Diane poured milk for Tucker. "Eat, eat everybody," she said. "Before it gets ice cold."

"What a ditz," Mallory whispered in my ear as she leaned over to put a milk glass in front of me.

On the other side of Cooper, Brian yanked a claw off his lobster. Then he cracked it open with a nutcracker. The shell made a sickening noise as it splintered. *Lobster Dinner Nutcracker Massacre.*

Across the table, Mallory was digging around inside her lobster claw with a fork. She smiled at me. I smiled back, grabbed a claw and pulled.

It reminded me a little of biology lab, but at least it smelled better. I finally managed to dig out a chunk of lobster, dipped it in the yellow stuff and put it in my mouth. It tasted a lot like chewy butter. It could have been worse. I swallowed it and wiped my mouth off with my napkin, before Mom could remind me to.

For a while nobody said anything. There were just the sounds of people dissecting lobsters and eating them. Then Mom asked Brian something about his work, and it turned out he was the boring kind of lawyer who never goes to court and just does stuff with taxes and money. I wished somebody would ask Mallory a question so I could find out more about her, but the adults were too busy sharing stories about the IRS.

I was watching Mallory eat her salad, one

lettuce leaf at a time, when Mr. Decker said, "Hey! I hit the jackpot with this one. Look, eggs."

Liz's fork crashed onto her plate. "You mean it was going to have babies?"

"Not anymore," Tucker said. He pointed at Mr. Decker's lobster. "You cook them alive. They still have their eyes and their antennas and their stomachs and their brains—"

"Alive?" Liz looked at Mom.

"And," Tucker said, "when you put them in the water, it's really hot, and they sort of try to climb back out again."

"Tucker," Mallory and Brian said at the same time.

I set down my fork with a piece of lobster still speared to the end and pushed my plate a little farther away from me. The room was suddenly warmer than it had been before. I wondered if I could just excuse myself, find the bathroom, throw up, fix my hair, and maybe get back in time for dessert.

Next to me, Cooper poured his milk over what was left of his macaroni and cheese. Then he shoved the cup off the tray again. I bent down to pick it up, careful to keep my head out of his reach. Actually I was sort of glad to have something to do besides eat. The air felt cooler under the table, and I rested my cheek for a second against the table leg. I glanced around at all the feet.

Mr. Decker and my mom were holding hands under the table.

I jerked my head back up and looked at Mom. She was listening to Brian and sort of messing her fork around in her salad, the way she does. I looked at Mr. Decker. He was listening to Brian, too, smiling, and twirling the wine in his glass with his left hand. You couldn't even tell what they were doing under the table. Somehow it seemed worse than if they were doing it out where everybody could see.

"Jonah," Diane said.

I jumped and nearly knocked over my milk. "What?"

"Ellen's been telling me about the business you and your friend have."

"What?" I said again. I assumed she was still speaking English, but my brain seemed to be translating it into Klingon and then not telling any of the rest of me what it meant.

"What kind of business is it?" Mallory asked. She put her fork down and leaned her chin on her hands. Her hair swung forward, and she pushed it back behind her ear. She looked like I was about to say something incredibly interesting, and she didn't want to miss a single word.

"Ah . . . business? Our business?" Did I know about a business? She had the biggest blue eyes. "Birthday parties," I remembered, finally.

"Birthday parties?" She laughed and, under the table, I felt her foot brush against mine. "Sorry," I said, and I moved my foot back a little.

"Oh, don't be sorry," Diane said. "It sounds like a wonderful idea."

Mallory laughed.

I tried to stop thinking about my feet. "We help out at birthday parties," I said. "We help the mothers."

"Hope they're filling out the proper tax forms," Brian said, and Mom and Mr. Decker laughed.

Mallory ignored them. She was still looking at me. Her foot brushed the top of mine again, then stayed there, pressing down. Then it was gone.

"Well," Diane said. "I was thinking maybe you could help out at Tucker's party next week. You and your friend."

I shuffled my foot out, and Mallory's foot was right there. I stepped on it, quick. She grinned, and I grinned back and pulled my foot away.

"Five," Tucker said. "I'm going to be five."

Diane smiled. "Yes, you are. Such a big boy." She looked back at me, and I forced myself to look at her instead of at Mallory. "Mallory's going to help, too. I just thought . . ." She smiled at

Mallory. "Wouldn't it be nice to have professional help, Mal?"

"Mallory," Mallory said. Then she smiled at me. "It'd be great."

Her foot tromped on mine. I tried to get her back, but I missed. "Oh, well," I said. I kept looking at Diane. "We'd like to be there. I mean, work there. I mean, it'll be fine."

Mom put her hand on my arm. "Hadn't you better check with Amanda first?"

"Who?"

"Amanda," Mom said, slowly, drawing the name out. "Your business partner." Both her hands were back on the table.

I slid my foot back out, searching for Mallory's. I couldn't stop grinning. "It'll be fine, Mom. Amanda'll think it's fine."

I felt my foot bump against something, and I stepped down. "Ow!" Brian said, and he gave me a funny look.

"Sorry," I said and jerked my foot back.

Across the table, Mallory giggled. I put my head down so Brian couldn't see me laughing, too. I felt Mallory's foot brush mine, and I stepped on hers quick, before it could get away.

CHAPTER NINE

Water Fight

There was a message from Amanda on the answering machine when we got home: "Don't forget we have a job tomorrow. We'll pick you up at twelve thirty."

I *had* forgotten. Mrs. Norton's cousin's brother's neighbor or something. I sighed. I'd sort of been hoping to hang around. Maybe Mr. Decker would come over, and maybe he'd say something about Mallory. I really wanted to hear some more about Mallory.

But Amanda showed up at our house right on time. "The Hennesseys live just over on Trillium. I figured we could walk. It's such a nice day." I figured that meant her mother wouldn't drive us, but she was right. It was a nice day, one of those days when you could see Mount Hood and Mount St. Helens both, if you were in the right place.

It was warm, and Amanda was wearing a big white T-shirt and tight, stretchy black pants. It looked like she'd done something different with her hair, curled it or fluffed it or something, but I didn't know if I should say anything about it.

"Guess what?" I said as we started down the driveway. "I've got us a job. Next Saturday."

She looked really surprised. "You've got us a job?"

"Yeah. What's so amazing about that?"

She shrugged. "I didn't think you were really into this whole thing."

"Well, I am," I said. "I wouldn't keep doing it if I wasn't into it."

"Okay, okay," she said. "So where's this party at?"

"Mr. Decker's daughter's."

Amanda stopped right in the middle of the sidewalk. "Mr. Decker has a daughter? We're going to do Mr. Decker's daughter's birthday party? I don't believe it. This is great. Wait till I tell Jill and Shawna."

"No, no. It's Mr. Decker's daughter's kid's birthday."

I thought Amanda's jaw was going to hit the sidewalk. "Mr. Decker's daughter has a kid? Mr. Decker is a grandfather?"

"You sound just like Liz. She's got two kids, and we're doing the four-year-old's party. Or the five-year-old. He's going to be five."

"Mr. Decker's daughter has two kids?"

"Diane," I said. "Actually, we can probably just call her Diane."

"You call Mr. Decker's daughter Diane?"

"That's her name," I said.

Amanda frowned. "How do you even know Mr. Decker's daughter?"

My jaw dropped. I'd been so excited about working at Tucker's party, so I could get to see Mallory again, that I'd forgotten all about my mom and Mr. Decker.

Amanda just stood there, looking at me.

"It's sort of a long story," I said.

"Yeah." She nodded and kept on standing there, waiting.

I took a deep breath. My mind ran through every plausible lie I could think of, but I knew for sure somebody next Saturday would say something. I let my breath out. "If I tell you something, do you promise not to blab it all over the school?"

Amanda put her hands on her hips. "I do not blab things, Jonah Truman."

"Not even to Shawna. Or Jill. You're not going to tell anybody this, okay?"

"Okay. But I can't believe this secret is such a big deal."

"It's not a secret. Well, it is a secret, but it's not a big deal. My mother's going out with Mr. Decker."

I thought she was going to faint. Her knees sort of crumpled a little bit. Her eyes got as big as

Frisbees. Then she clapped her hands on top of her head and walked around in a circle. I wished Mom could see her. I wished she could see how weird people act when they hear stuff like this. Finally Amanda said, "Jonah. Jonah. This is great. This is just incredible."

I started walking. "It's not that great."

Amanda trotted to catch up with me. "What's so bad about it? I think Mr. Decker is nice."

"And cute," I said.

"And cute," she said. "He and your mom probably look really cute together." She snapped her fingers. "That's the car that's been in your driveway!"

I shrugged. We crossed Ivy and started down Magnolia. Amanda kept saying, "Mr. Decker, Mr. Decker," under her breath. She turned toward me. "If you call his daughter Diane, what do you call Mr. Decker?"

"Mr. Decker." I thought about telling her what Liz called him, but I was afraid she'd just die right there in the middle of the street.

"How did you meet his daughter?"

"We went over there for dinner."

"You had dinner at Mr. Decker's? What's his house look like? I've always wondered what his house would look like."

"It was Diane's house. We went to her house."

"The two families together?" Amanda turned so far toward me she almost had to walk sideways.

"It was no big deal, Amanda."

"Well, I just hope you guys made a good impression, for your mom's sake."

I stopped. "Nobody needs to make an impression."

"I don't know." Amanda shook her head and her hair bounced around her ears. "My aunt Judy was going to marry this guy, and my mom and dad talked her out of it because they couldn't stand his family." Amanda tilted her head to one side and wagged her finger at a bush beside the sidewalk. " 'Judy,' my mom would say, 'imagine spending every Christmas with those people. You'll never have to bring a fruitcake. They *are* fruitcakes.' "

I frowned at her. "Nobody's marrying anybody, Amanda. They're just going out."

She kicked at a dandelion fluff in the grass. "You never know, Jonah. Your mom's not getting any younger. She's facing a lonely old age."

She was starting to make me sort of mad. I leaned close and looked up into her face. "She's not marrying him, Amanda. How many times do I have to tell you?"

"Okay," she said.

"Okay," I said. I started walking again, and she jogged a little to keep up.

"Five-year-olds," she said, after about half a block. "We've never done a party for five-year-olds."

"Diane seemed to think it would be all right. And Mallory will be there." I smiled. Just saying her name made me smile.

"Mallory? Who's he?"

"She. She's Brian's daughter. Diane's husband. He was married before or something."

Amanda pursed up her lips. "How old is Mallory?"

"Our age. She goes to Kimmel. You'll like her a lot. She's really great." I thought about the feet under the table and—I couldn't help it—I laughed out loud.

"What's so funny?"

"Oh, nothing. It was just something . . . never mind." I smiled and shook my head. "I just know you'll like Mallory. She's really—"

"Great," Amanda finished. "I know. You said that." She was staring at me. I just couldn't stop smiling, I guess. "Do we have to split the money with her?"

I stopped smiling. "I don't know." I hadn't even thought about the money. In fact, I hadn't even mentioned money to Diane.

Amanda looked like she was going to say something, but then she just shook her head. She started walking faster. "We'd better hurry up," she said, over her shoulder. "We're going to be late."

There was no tea at the Hennesseys' party. When each kid got there, Amanda painted his face green and black for camouflage. Then he was sent to boot camp in the backyard. Everybody had to do exercises and crawl through hula hoops and swing across the jungle gym. I got to blow a whistle and yell a lot. When everybody had won their dog tags, we divided up into teams. I was captain of the Green team and Amanda was captain of the Blue team. We split up and played capture-the-flag all over the neighborhood, and everybody was armed with water guns.

My team had captured almost half of the Blue team, when I spotted Amanda, alone and unguarded, behind the Robinsons' garden shed. I had a pretty good idea that she was carrying their flag, because I knew Amanda wouldn't trust it to one of the kids. I hadn't trusted *ours* to a kid.

I snuck up behind her. "Who goes there?" I shouted, as loud and deep as I could.

She jumped about five feet straight up and spun around. I shot her, right in the chest. I'd just filled my water gun, and I pumped up a lot of pressure, and I totally soaked her.

"Ha!" I shouted. "Got you good!" I was backing up, trying to get out of range.

But she didn't move toward me. She just

stood there, staring down at her dripping shirt. I could see her bra through the wet material. I'd never known Amanda wore a bra.

"You jerk, Jonah Truman!" She threw her gun at me. I jumped back, and it clattered on the ground next to my feet.

"What?" I said. "What did I do?"

"You got me all wet!" she shouted. The wet shirt made a little sucking sound as she pulled it away from her skin.

Two of her team came around the side of the shed, followed by some of the guys from my side. They stopped spraying each other when they saw us. They all came over and stood in a little semicircle behind me, and we all stared at Amanda.

"Getting people wet is the point of the game," I said. "That's how the game works, Amanda." I looked at the kids, and they all nodded.

One of them whispered something, and they all started giggling. Amanda glared at them. One of them saluted her, and they all laughed even harder. Amanda folded her arms across her chest and turned back toward me. "I bet you wouldn't get Katherine wet. Or what's-her-face."

I frowned. "Who?"

"You are so dumb, Jonah." She took a big, shaky breath, and, for one awful second, I was afraid she was starting to cry. But when she looked at me again, she just looked mad. "I am sick and tired of being treated like one of the guys. Do you understand that? I am not a guy."

"No duh," one of the kids said.

Amanda ignored him. She took a step closer to me. I could see that the bra had lace or something on the straps. "And don't you dare," she said, "mention a word of this to Kevin Martinez."

I forced myself to look at her face instead of her chest. "Okay," I said. Believe me. The last thing I was going to do was tell Kevin about *this.*

"Good," Amanda said, and she stomped off toward the Hennesseys' house.

I bent down and picked up her water gun. One of my guys tugged on my sleeve. "Does this mean we win?"

I shook my head. "She's still got the flag."

CHAPTER TEN

Just Another Great Day

When the party was over, Amanda left the house so fast I couldn't catch up with her. Not that I was going to go chasing her down the sidewalk, anyway. It hadn't been my fault that I'd gotten her all wet. I'd just been doing my job.

Mom was sitting at the dining-room table, correcting papers. "How was the party?"

"Fine." I went into the kitchen. There was nothing in the refrigerator but some yogurt and carrots and juice. I went back into the living room. "There's never anything to eat around here."

"How about lobster?" She looked up at me. "We could always have lobster."

"Yeah," I said. "That was great."

She laughed and drew a big purple star at the top of one of the papers. "What did you think of last night, anyway?"

"I had a good time," I said. I knew my face was getting red, but I didn't care. "It was fun. I liked it."

"I liked it, too." She shook her head, muttered, “Oh, Brandon,” and wrote *See me* in purple at the top of the next paper. “Bob was really pleased at how well you and Mallory got along. He said he’d never seen Mallory look so relaxed.”

I knew my face could probably light an entire subdivision. “She was okay,” I said.

“Well,” Mom said. She looked up at me again. “Isn’t it nice that every cloud has a silver lining?”

I didn’t know what she was talking about, but I said, “Yeah. I guess.”

She drew another purple star. “I saw Amanda go by about ninety miles an hour. I thought you guys were walking together.”

“We were,” I said.

Mom raised her eyebrows. “Is something wrong? Did you have a fight?”

Just a water fight. “Not exactly.” I shook my head. “I think Amanda’s going through one of those stages or something.”

Mom laughed. “I know how she feels.”

I wasn’t sure exactly how mad Amanda was, but by Monday morning I was worried that she might be mad enough to tell everybody at school about Mom and Mr. Decker. I looked for her, so I could apologize for getting her wet or treating her like a guy or whatever it was I’d done. But I missed her before language arts, and she was sitting with a bunch of girls at lunch, and then I was late for band because I couldn't find my music and . . . well, by then it was so late, I figured she hadn't told anybody anything, and I sort of relaxed.

Anyway, I was spending a lot of time thinking about Mallory. I imagined her maybe transfering to Walt Morey. I imagined eating lunch with her and walking down the halls with her. I imagined horrible extraterrestrials landing on the front lawn and breaking into the school, right in the middle of social studies, and me throwing myself in between Mallory and their phasers and saving her life.

It was a great week. Probably the best time I'd had at school since, maybe, fourth grade. I made a touchdown in flag football during intramurals. I got an A on the paper I'd written about the Civil War. And Mrs. Fletcher never called on me once in algebra.

I felt so good that on Wednesday, when Katherine Chang smiled at me outside language arts, I said, "Hi, Katherine. How's it going?" without thinking about it or messing it up or anything.

At dinner on Wednesday night, Mom said, "Bob's coming over this evening. He and I are going to grab a cup of coffee or something at the mall."

"Okay," I said.

Liz looked at me. "Aren't you going to go upstairs and play your horn really loud?"

I ignored her.

When the doorbell rang about an hour later, I shouted, "I'll get it!"

"Hi Jonah," Mr. Decker said. For a second, I almost didn't recognize him. He was wearing jeans and a sweatshirt. And he'd cut his hair so it didn't stick up so much.

"Hi," I said. "Come on in." I smiled at him like I was glad to see him. And I was glad to see him. I liked Mr. Decker. Mr. Decker was okay. If it hadn't been for him, we would have never gone to his daughter's for dinner, and I would never have met Mallory. My whole life had changed because of Mr. Decker.

I led him into the living room. Liz came running in and sort of did her twirling and squealing thing, and even that was okay tonight. I smiled at Mr. Decker and shook my head, and he smiled back.

"Why don't you sit down," I said.

"Yeah," Liz said. "Sit down. I want to show you my downtown Portland project. I made Portlandia out of Play-Doh."

"Well," Mr. Decker said, "I know your mom wants to get going. Maybe just for a minute."

So he sat down, and Liz showed him the statue, and it was nice. I mean, really. It was okay.

Mr. Decker looked different somehow, sitting

there on the couch. Not like I'd imagined he'd look. And it wasn't just that he'd lost the red sweater and the awful ties. He just looked . . . well, he just looked almost like a regular person. I was glad that he got up so fast when Mom came in, giving her this big smile and tugging at his pants leg where it had gotten stuck in his sneaker. I started thinking that having Mr. Decker around might not be such a bad thing after all.

Liz and I stood at the door and watched them go down the walk. "Have a good time," I said. And I meant that, too.

Kevin stopped by my locker first thing Thursday morning. He was wearing a T-shirt that said "All reality is virtual."

"Nice shirt," I said.

"My dad got it at a software conference. Can you spend the night tomorrow night?"

"Uh, I'm not sure, Kev." I'd sort of wanted to spend the night putting hot compresses on my face and figuring out what I was going to wear to Tucker's party. "I'll have to check with my mom."

Jerry and Travis and Brad were walking down the far side of the hall. Travis was shoving Jerry into the path of people going the other way, and they were laughing at the dirty looks they were getting. I stuck up my hand. "Hey, Brad. I have something for you."

They crossed the hall to our side. I dug in my locker and found the *Penthouse* I'd finally brought back with me that morning. I tossed it at Brad. "Here." I said, "It's all yours."

He caught it and jammed it into his binder. "Smooth move, Jonah," he said, looking up and down the hall. "I can't take this to science. Mr. Jacobi's checking our notebooks today." He ran off toward his locker.

I laughed.

Travis was leaning against the locker next to mine. "You're sure you're done with it now, Jonah," he said. He looked at Jerry. "I bet he didn't even open it."

I ignored him. I was feeling too good to let Travis get to me. I slammed my locker shut, spun the lock, and turned to go.

Amanda was coming down the hall. She waved her hand when she saw me. "I need to talk to you," she said. A little bit of the good feeling drained out of me. All of a sudden, I wondered if I should have tried harder to apologize on Monday.

I took a step toward her, thinking maybe I could head her off, or at least get her to keep her voice down, in case she was going to start yelling or something. But Travis moved with me, and everybody else sort of followed. Amanda walked right up to the whole bunch of us.

She gave me a big smile. "Hi Jonah," she said. "I just wanted to know how we get to this job on Saturday."

"They're picking us up," I said. I tried to talk fast, so maybe no one else would understand what I was saying. I moved to the right, to get past her. "One o'clock, at my house."

She shifted to block me. "And the money?"

"The money's okay. The money's fine." I'd pay her myself, if I had to. I'd pay her double, if she'd just move out of my way. I stepped to the left.

She blocked me again. "And I wanted to tell you that we have another job. A week from Saturday. We're hot. We may have to hire help." She looked at Kevin and smiled.

"What money?" Kevin said. "What job?" He looked at me, but before I could say anything, Amanda said, "Didn't Jonah tell you? We're working together. We have a birthday party service. You know, helping the parents with the games, entertaining the kids, stuff like that."

Travis laughed, his loudest, most obnoxious laugh. "Isn't that special?" he said. He nudged Jerry with his elbow, and Jerry laughed, too.

"We're making a lot of money," I said. "For the trip to the beach."

Travis and Jerry looked at each other and grinned. They didn't say anything. Kevin was staring at me.

"It's a business," I said to him. "There aren't any lawns to mow now. You know I need the money."

"The theme this time is the circus," Amanda said. "But don't worry. No clown suits." She smiled at Kevin again. "You ever have a party with a theme?"

Kevin shrugged. "I've got four brothers. I'm lucky if they remember my birthday."

Amanda nodded. "We always just played musical chairs and pin-the-tail-on-the-donkey. I don't know about themes." She shifted her bag to the other shoulder. "I gotta go. See you." She waved at Kevin, then she took off down the hall.

I started to edge toward algebra.

"So," Travis said, slowly, "is this serious?"

"Of course it's serious," I said. "I told you, we're making a lot of money."

"Does Katherine know about it?" Jerry asked, and he and Travis grinned.

"About what?" I said.

"About this thing with you and Amanda," Jerry said.

"We'd better get going, guys," Kevin said. "We're going to be late."

"She sure is tall," Travis said. He put his hand up above my head. "You're going to need a ladder, man."

"Look," I said. "There is nothing between me and Moose Matzinger. Get it?"

"Oh, we get it, Jonah," Travis said, and he nudged Jerry again, and they both laughed.

The good feeling was gone completely. I was mad now. Mad at Amanda. Mad at these two jerks. Mad at Kevin for just standing there with his mouth open. "Come on," I said to him. "We are late."

Jerry snapped his fingers. "Oh, Jonah. I nearly forgot. I was going to tell you." He paused, and looked at Travis and Kevin, making sure they were listening, too. "I saw your mom and Mr. Decker at the mall last night."

I froze right where I was.

"The mall?" Kevin said.

"Jonah, Jonah." Travis was shaking his head. "Have you been a bad boy? Has Mr. Decker been talking to your mother about you?"

"Yeah, right," I said. I tried to laugh, but it didn't come out right. "He must have run into her at the mall."

Jerry was shaking his head. "I don't know. They looked pretty happy to me. They were smiling and talking." He raised his eyebrows. "Holding hands."

The insides of my stomach twisted and churned. I'd told her this would happen. I'd warned her.

Travis was grinning. He leaned close, and I could smell the gum he was chewing. I could see the zit nestled up against the side of his nose. "Jonah," he said. "Does Mr. Decker have the hots for your mother?"

Before I even knew what it was doing, my right hand flew out, and I hit him. I hit him as hard as I could.

CHAPTER ELEVEN

Bob

My fist brushed across Travis's chin and banged into his teeth. Pain shot straight up my arm.

Travis clamped his hand over his mouth. He backed a step away from me.

About fifty kids materialized in a ring around us. "What's going on?" somebody said. "Fight," Jerry said, and farther back, somebody yelled, "Fight!"

Travis took his hand away from his mouth. A bright trickle of blood ran down his lip. "You're going to regret this, Truman," he said, but he didn't move toward me. He just stood there, glaring at me.

My whole hand ached, and my middle finger was throbbing. I'd cut the knuckle open, probably on Travis's front teeth. Blood was dripping slowly toward my fingernail.

"Hit him, Trav," somebody said. "Hit him back."

Travis looked around the circle. He looked back at me. He frowned. He looked bigger than he had a minute ago. Bigger and angrier and meaner.

I tried to take a step back, but kids were so close around us, I couldn't go anywhere. Somebody shoved me, and I stumbled closer to Travis. He put his hands up, and I put mine up, too, like I'd seen guys do in movies.

"All right. Break it up."

One minute, the hall was full of kids. The next second, it was just Travis and me, standing there in front of the lockers, all alone. Even Kevin was gone.

Mr. Decker and Mr. Graham, the tech teacher, were coming down the hall, fast.

Travis turned and took a step.

"Hold it, Travis."

He stopped and turned around.

Mr. Decker stood about three feet away from us. He put his hands on his hips, inside his suit jacket. He glanced at Mr. Graham. "I can handle this, Sandy." Mr. Graham nodded and went back the way he'd come. His sneakers squeaked on the floor.

Mr. Decker looked from me to Travis and back to me.

"He hit me," Travis said. He pointed at me. His lip had stopped bleeding, but there was still a thin trail of blood. "He hit me, and I wasn't even doing anything."

Mr. Decker looked at me. I didn't say anything.

"Is that what happened, Jonah?" Mr. Decker's voice echoed in the empty hallway.

I shrugged.

Mr. Decker sighed. "I want to see both of you in my office. Right now." He pointed down the hallway, as if Travis and I didn't know where his office was.

I walked past him, sucking on my knuckle. The blood tasted sharp and metallic.

Mrs. Gifaldi, the secretary, glanced up as we filed past her desk. She looked bored and tired, as if bloody kids went past her desk all day long. Mr. Decker stopped and said something to her. I wondered if he was telling her to call my mother, but then I decided I didn't care.

I'd never actually been inside Mr. Decker's office. There was a desk covered with folders and computer manuals. There was a table in the corner with a computer that was running a screen saver. There were shelves with lots of hardbound books and binders on them. Behind the desk, on the wall, there was a big picture of Diane and Brian and Tucker and Cooper. They were all wearing white turtlenecks and black pants. They were all smiling.

Mr. Decker pulled the door shut behind us, and the room seemed smaller and darker.

A chair faced the desk. Travis went over and

slumped into it, like it was his chair, just waiting for him to show up. He crossed his arms.

Mr. Decker pulled an identical chair out from the computer. "Sit down, Jonah," he said.

I sat and watched him go behind the desk and settle into the big chair behind it. I thought about my fist smacking up against Travis's mouth, and I was glad I'd done it. I wished I could do it again.

Mr. Decker looked at Travis, who was checking out a hole in the knee of his jeans. Mr. Decker looked at me. I looked right back at him, staring right into his eyes.

He blinked first and looked back at Travis. "Your lip has stopped bleeding," he said. "Are your teeth okay?"

Travis opened his mouth wide. "Oo ay ook okay?"

Mr. Decker leaned closer across the desk. "They look okay."

Travis stuck his thumb into his mouth and tried to wiggle his front teeth. He sucked saliva back in, then said, "I guess they feel okay. But my lip hurts. Look." He peeled his bottom lip back carefully so Mr. Decker and I could see the cut. It wasn't very big, but the lip was red and swollen. It must have hit against his bottom teeth.

Mr. Decker got up and crossed back behind us to the door. He opened it and said, "Mrs. Gifaldi, would you please get us an ice pack," and then he shut the door again and came back to his chair.

Neither Travis nor I moved or said anything. I stared at the picture of Brian and Diane.

"So." Mr. Decker leaned back in his chair, and it creaked underneath him. "Just what happened out there?"

"He hit me," Travis said. He jerked his thumb in my direction. "He hit me right in the mouth."

Mr. Decker looked at me. "Travis says you hit him, Jonah."

What did the guy think, I was deaf? I kept staring at the picture. I wondered how they'd gotten Cooper to sit still and smile like that.

Mr. Decker leaned forward and rested his arms on the desk. "Jonah?" he said.

"I guess I did that," I said. "I guess I hit him." I looked down at my knuckle. It had stopped bleeding, too. There was only the thin, red line of the cut now.

There was a knock at the door. Travis glanced back, but Mr. Decker and I just sat there. Finally Mr. Decker said, "Come in."

Mrs. Gifaldi set a frozen sponge in a plastic bag on the desk. It was a green sponge, just like the one we had on our sink at home. "There you go," Mrs. Gifaldi said, and she smiled, like she'd just put a plate of cookies in front of us. She held up a pair of plastic gloves and raised her eyebrows at Mr. Decker. He shook his head. "I don't think I need them." Mrs. Gifaldi nodded and closed the door behind her.

Mr. Decker handed the plastic bag to Travis. Travis pressed it against his lower lip. "Thanks," he mumbled.

Mr. Decker sat there watching him. "Why do you think you hit him, Jonah?" He didn't look at me. He kept watching Travis.

"I don't *think* I hit him. I know I hit him," I said.

Mr. Decker looked straight at me again. He sat up a little taller in his chair. Anger flashed across his face, so fast I would have missed it if I hadn't been looking for it. Then his face settled back into that calm, "Mister Rogers" look. I smiled. One point for me.

"And why exactly did you hit him, Jonah?"

I shrugged. "Beats me." I looked at Travis and laughed. "Get it? Beats me?" I laughed again and stretched my legs out toward the desk. I shook my head, like I couldn't believe how funny this all was.

Travis wiggled as far away from me as he could get and still stay in the chair. His eyes above the sponge looked worried.

Mr. Decker was frowning now. He looked like maybe he was going to say something to me, but instead, he said, "Travis. Do you have any idea why Jonah might have hit you?"

Travis sat forward in his chair. He put the sponge back on the desk. "I was just standing there, minding my own business. I wasn't doing anything."

Mr. Decker smiled. He picked up a pen and put it back down. "Travis, we both know that your definition of not doing anything is not the same as my definition."

They both smiled and sat back in their chairs a little bit. I had thrown them off there for a second, but now they were on familiar ground.

Travis picked at a loose thread around the hole in his jeans. "You know, Mr. Decker," he said, "I think this may all have just been a mistake. I may have said something that made Jonah a little angry, and Jonah may have sort of hit me, but, well, I'm willing to forget all about it." He held up his hand like Mr. Decker had been about to say something. "I know you can't condone violence, Mr. Decker, and I can't either. But, this once, well, I think we should all make an exception." He turned to me and stuck out his hand. "Let's shake on it, Jonah," he said.

Mr. Decker raised an eyebrow at me. "What do you think about that?"

"Gee," I said. "I looked at Travis's outstretched hand. I looked at Mr. Decker. I leaned back in my chair. I steepled my fingers and rested my chin on top of them. "I just don't know . . . Bob."

Travis gasped. Mr. Decker's eyebrow looked like it was permanently stuck in the "up" position.

"Bob," I said again, "I just don't think it was a mistake." I dropped my hands, and the metal arms of the chair felt cool against my sweaty palms. "A mistake would have been, like, if I'd been aiming for a locker and hit Travis instead. But I was aiming for Travis. I was definitely aiming right for him."

"Jonah," Travis said, under his breath.

Mr. Decker had picked up the pen again. He was tapping, tapping it on one of the folders.

"Do you really want to know why I hit Travis, Bob? I mean, do you want to know just exactly what we were talking about before I decided to punch him right in the mouth?"

"Jo-nah," Travis said, in a louder voice. I looked at him. "Are you crazy?" he whispered. I smiled and turned back to Mr. Decker.

His mouth was pinched into a hard, white line.

"*Do* you want to know?" I asked again.

"Certainly," he said, and the word barely got past his lips.

"No," Travis said. He stood up and took a step toward the desk. "No. Take my word for it, Mr. Decker. Jonah's nuts. Jonah's gone crazy."

I stood up, too. I put my hands flat on the desk top. "Travis and I were talking, Bob," I said.

"We were talking about whether or not you . . . whether or not you . . ." I couldn't get the words out.

Travis shoved into me and pushed me to one side. "I did *not* say that you have the hots for his mother."

"You did, too." I shoved him back, using the backs of my arms and my elbows.

"I did not." He pushed against my chest, and I had to step back. My foot hit the garbage can and knocked it over.

Mr. Decker stood up and leaned across the desk. "Stop it! Both of you! Stop it right now!" He was yelling, and I knew Mrs. Gifaldi could hear him through the closed door. Travis and I both froze where we were.

Mr. Decker took a deep breath and let it out, very slowly. He pointed at me. "Sit down." His voice was very quiet now. I sat.

"Travis," Mr. Decker said. "I want to talk to Jonah alone." He scribbled something on a piece of paper and slid it across the desk. "This will get you into your class."

Travis nodded. He grabbed the piece of paper and got out of there, fast.

That left just me and Bob.

CHAPTER TWELVE

"I Never Thought You Had It in You"

Mr. Decker sank back down into his chair. He ran his hand over his hair, and the gray curls flattened and then sprang back up. Neither one of us said anything. I could hear the computer humming in the corner and the sound of somebody talking to Mrs. Gifaldi outside the door. I took a breath and let it out, and it came out kind of shaky. For some reason, I thought about Mrs. Palmer teaching us to spell "principal" back in third grade. "Just remember," she'd said, "the principal is your pal."

Mr. Decker picked up the pen again, studied it, then put it back down. I looked down at his hands, resting on the surface of the desk. The fingers of his right hand started tapping up and down. He looked down, too, and his fingers stopped.

"I think, Jonah," he said, and his voice was so sudden, I jumped. "I think this is something you need to talk about with your mother." He cleared his throat. "These feelings," he said.

I didn't say anything.

"This anger," he said, as though he were finishing a thought.

I looked down at my own hands. You could hardly even see the cut.

"Travis was right, of course." His voice was firmer and stronger. I knew he was looking at me. "I can't condone the use of violence. No matter how strong the provocation. Violence never solved anything," he said, and now his voice sounded like the usual Mr. Decker. Mr. Decker the principal. Not Mr. Decker who sat on my couch in jeans and a sweatshirt.

I nodded. Maybe if I did something to show I was listening, he'd let me out of there.

"But I do expect you to talk to your mother. She wants to know how you're feeling. Jonah?"

I forced myself to look at him. I kind of had to tilt my head to one side, but I did it.

"I'm trusting you to talk to your mother when you get home."

In your dreams, I thought. "Okay," I said, and my own voice sounded hoarse and far away.

Mr. Decker stood up and came around the desk. I stood up, too. For a second, I thought he was going to put his hand on my shoulder, but he handed me a hall pass instead. "This could be all for the best," he said. "Getting things out into the open." His mouth smiled, even though his eyes still had that worried look.

"I guess," I said, and walked out of the office.

Mrs. Gifaldi's desk was empty. I pushed through the glass doors out into the hall. I'd wadded the pass up in my hand. I couldn't even remember what class I was supposed to be in. All of a sudden, I wanted to turn around and go back into the office. I wanted to ask him exactly what was going on with him and my mother. But I knew he was standing there in his doorway, watching me. I turned to the right and went around the corner.

Travis was leaning against the wall. I sidestepped, just in case he was going to start shoving me again. But he was grinning. "Jeez," he said, "I couldn't believe you in there."

"Get lost," I said, but he fell into step beside me.

"What did he do to you? What did he say?"

"He told me I need to talk to my mother."

Travis laughed and slapped a locker. "I can't believe it. *Bob,*" he said, and he made the name sound longer than it really was. "I never thought you had it in you, Jonah. I mean, I always thought you were a total geek. But you're not. You're okay." He slapped me on the back.

I winced and moved away a little.

Classroom doors started opening on both sides of the hall, and kids came pouring out. Travis stepped closer to me and put his arm across my shoulder. “Don’t worry,” he said, quietly. “I’ll tell Jerry to keep his mouth shut.” He winked at me, then slapped my back again. “I gotta go to art,” he said. He disappeared into the crowd.

Kevin came out of the bathroom. He looked at me and frowned. “Are you okay?”

I shrugged. “Travis says I am. I guess I must be.”

“Are you really working with Amanda?”

“Yeah.”

“Are we still going to mow lawns?”

I looked at him. “Believe me, Kevin, I would much rather mow lawns. Mowing lawns is easy compared to birthday parties.”

He nodded. Then he said, “Why did Jerry make up that story about your mom and Mr. Decker?”

I sighed. “It’s not a story.”

“It’s not?”

“No. It’s true.”

Kevin nodded his head slowly. “Weird,” he said, finally.

“No kidding,” I said.

Nobody else mentioned my mom or Mr. Decker for the rest of the day. There was some whispering that stopped when I came in, but that was about it. People seemed a lot more impressed by the fact that I’d hit Travis.

When school was over, Amanda caught up

with me on the sidewalk. She was out of breath. "Jill said you hit Travis Hunter and gave him a black eye."

"I don't really feel like talking about it, Amanda."

"Did you give Travis a black eye?"

"No."

Amanda nodded. "I didn't think you did."

"I hit him in the mouth and cut his lip."

Amanda's eyes widened, but she didn't say anything. I walked a little faster, and she kept up with me.

"I was afraid it was my fault."

I stopped and looked at her. She was looking at her toe, making circles on the pavement. "Why would it be your fault?"

"You know." She took a deep breath. "I was afraid Travis made fun of you because of the birthday parties." She kept looking at her foot. "And stuff," she said.

I shook my head, but she wasn't looking at me. "No," I said. "It wasn't because of that." I remembered that I'd called her Moose in front of Travis and Jerry and Kevin. "I'm sorry I got you wet the other day."

"Oh, that." She wiggled around in her jacket like she had a bug stuck down her back. "That was dumb. I was acting dumb." She looked at me. "I guess I was a little jealous."

"Oh." I wasn't sure what she'd been jealous of. My team? My way with a squirt gun? "Yeah," I said.

She stepped off the sidewalk to let a bunch of kids walk past. Then she moved closer to me and said, in a quiet voice, "Jill said Travis said your mother's in love with Mr. Adamson."

I laughed. My mother had better taste than that. "What did you say?"

"I said that was ridiculous. Actually, I said your mother has better taste."

I laughed again. She tucked some loose strands of hair back into her braid. "Mrs. Hennessey was a total wacko, wasn't she? I couldn't believe that whole party. I mean, who has a war at a birthday party?"

"It was pretty crazy, all right," I said.

"I hope the party on Saturday is better."

"Oh, it will be," I said. "I'm sure of it."

The house was empty when I got home. There was a note fastened to the refrigerator with the "World's Best Teacher" magnet. *Taking Liz to the dentist.*

I heaved a sigh of relief. Thank goodness for Liz's teeth. Sometime I'd have to talk to Mom. I knew Mr. Decker would tell her about what had happened at school. Adults always tell each other stuff like that. It would be better if I talked to her first, but I'd have to pick the right time. And the right story.

I got a container of cherry yogurt out of the refrigerator and dug in the drawer for a spoon. The answering machine's message light was on. I pushed rewind and hit the play button.

There was the beep, and then a girl's voice said, "Oh, no . . ." She giggled, and it sounded like somebody else said something and she said, "Answering machine," and there was a lot more giggling and whispering.

I put the yogurt down and turned the volume up.

"So!" The voice boomed out, and I turned the volume back down. "So, this is Stacey? I was wondering if Jonah . . ." There was even more giggling. "Jonah Truman? I was wondering if he could call me back." She recited a phone number, and I wrote it down on the "World's Greatest Teacher" notepad.

I looked at the number. I wrote "Stacey?" above it. The only Stacey I knew was in ninth grade now, and he was a boy.

I grabbed the phone and, quick, before I could change my mind, I dialed. As soon as my finger hit the last number, I started to hang up, but someone answered before I could.

"Hello?" It was definitely the same voice.

"Uh. May I please speak to Stacey?"

I heard her say, "It's him!" with her hand over the mouthpiece. Then, more clearly, she said, "This is me."

"Oh." I could hear loud breathing, like maybe two people were breathing close to the phone. "I think you left a message on our answering machine."

"Move *over,*" she said. Then, "Not you. I mean, you don't have to move." She laughed.

"Uh . . ." I wasn't sure how to tell her that I didn't know who she was.

"Actually," she said, "you don't even know me. I go to Kimmel."

"Oh." My heart started pounding. I was afraid they could hear it. "Yeah?"

"Yeah." There was talking in the background, and the phone got bumped against something. "And . . ." She was shouting. "And Mallory Beckwith wants to know if you like her!"

There was a scream close to my ear, and then somebody banged the phone down.

I hung up and just stood there, staring at the sticky notes stuck on the cupboard door. The phone rang. I let it ring one more time, then I picked it up. "Hello?"

"Hi. This is Mallory."

"Hi," I said. I started to sit down, then I stood up again.

"I just wanted you to know that I had nothing to do with that last phone call."

"Oh."

"It was all Stacey's idea. Stacey is so immature. Just ignore her."

"Oh," I said again.

"So, anyway. I guess I'll see you this Saturday? At Tucker's party?"

"Oh," I said, and I slapped myself on the forehead. Get a grip, Jonah. "Right," I said.

"It'll be great to see you again."

"Yeah. I mean, yes. I mean, it'll be great to see you."

"Well. Bye."

"Bye."

There was silence, then she said, "Are you still there?"

"No." I hung up, fast. Then I smacked my hand on the table. "All right!" I said.

The back door opened, and Mom and Liz came in. "Well," Mom said, "how was school?"

"Great," I said. "Absolutely great."

CHAPTER THIRTEEN

Pirates!

Amanda was at our house at one o'clock on Saturday. I had spent most of the morning and the night before trying on different clothes. I finally settled on the Seattle Seahawks jersey and the black jeans Mom had bought me for Easter. Of course, switching shirts had messed up my hair.

"I'll be there in a minute!" I shouted down the stairs as I crossed the hall to the bathroom. I heard Liz say something, and I heard Amanda laugh.

I fixed my hair and did a quick zit check. The medicine and hot compresses I'd been doing all week had made the one on my chin almost disappear. All in all, the effect was not too bad. I tried a smile. "Hi Mallory," I said. I tried a more serious, sincere sort of look. "Hi Mal," I said.

"Brian's here!" Mom shouted. "Get a move on, Jonah."

I smoothed my hair down quick, one last time, tried one last smile and went downstairs.

Amanda was wearing the jeans skirt again

and a cowboy shirt and a pair of boots I didn't remember seeing before. She looked me up and down, but she didn't say anything.

"You've got a stain," Liz said. "Right there," and she poked me in the chest.

She was right. There was a little yellow blob under the hawk's eye. "I gotta change," I said.

Mom grabbed my sleeve. "Oh, no, you don't," she said and shoved me out the door.

Amanda got into the front seat of Brian's BMW, so I climbed in back. Brian introduced himself to Amanda, then looked back over his shoulder. "Good to see you, Jonah." He smiled at Amanda. "And good to see the reinforcements. We're going to need all the help we can get to battle those pirates."

"Pirates?" Amanda and I said at the same time.

Brian was backing down the driveway. He shut one eye. "Aye, maties. We're going to have a houseful of scurvy knaves." I hoped he wouldn't hit the mailbox, driving with only one eye.

I looked around me. Real leather upholstery, and there wasn't a candy wrapper or a McDonald's cup anywhere. I thought about Mallory maybe sitting right here where I was sitting now. My palms started getting sweaty. I rubbed them on my knees so I wouldn't get sweat on the seats.

Diane was tying black balloons to their mailbox when we pulled up. There was a big Jolly Roger pinned to the front door. As we climbed the steps, the door opened, and Tucker charged straight at us, a plastic sword out in front of him, screaming at the top of his lungs.

Amanda and I stepped apart, and Tucker ran right out onto the front porch and into his father's legs. He was still screaming. Brian picked him up. "He's just a little excited," Brian said.

Cooper wobbled out of the living room. He took one look at us, and then he started screaming, too.

Diane pushed past Brian and picked Cooper up. "It's okay, honey. Look. They're not baby-sitters." Cooper screamed even louder. "He thinks you're baby-sitters!" Diane shouted, smiling.

"Walk the plank!" Tucker shouted, and he took a swipe at Brian's head with his sword.

Amanda leaned over and whispered in my ear. "No way can they be paying us enough."

Mallory came in from the kitchen. I straightened up and forced myself to keep my hands away from my hair.

"Hi," Mallory said.

"Hi Mallory," I said, and I smiled. I decided not to try the serious, sincere look just yet.

"Mallory is Brian's daughter," Diane said. "She's going to be helping us out, too."

"I know," Amanda said. She smiled and Mallory smiled back.

Diane handed Cooper into Brian's other arm. "Why don't you start *Peter Pan* on the VCR, and I'll tell these guys the game plan."

Brian carried the kids, both of them still yelling, up the stairs.

Diane looked at the three of us. She ran her fingers through her hair, and it all fell back into exactly the same place. "Right," she said. She pulled Mallory over closer to me. I felt my hand brush against Mallory's arm. It tried to jerk away, but I made it stay there. And her arm stayed there, too. I took a deep breath and let it out, real slowly, so as not to disturb anything. I wondered if I could just stand there for the rest of my life, in Diane's front hall, with the tips of my fingers brushing against Mallory's sleeve.

" . . . is that okay with you, Jonah?" Diane asked.

"Sure," I said. "That sounds great." I had no idea what she was talking about.

"So." Diane ticked off on her fingers. "Amanda's doing hats and eye patches. Mallory's on the bread-stick sword fights. And Jonah's doing face painting."

"That does sound great," Amanda said. She was grinning.

"Then I'll need Amanda and Jonah to run the treasure hunt—it's all set up in the backyard—thank goodness it isn't raining, right?" She smiled at all of us. Mallory rolled her eyes. "And," Diane continued, "Mallory and I will get the hot dogs ready and the cake and ice cream." She turned toward Mallory and whispered, "Shall we show them the cake, Mal?"

"Mallory," Mallory said, and she stepped away from Diane and closer to me.

The dining room was decorated with more black balloons and Jolly Rogers. The table was covered with a black tablecloth. The cake sat in the middle.

"Wow," Amanda and I both said.

We'd seen a lot of cakes in the past few weeks, but this one . . . well, this one took the cake. There was a blue sea with a pirate ship and shark fins poking up out of the waves. There was an island with a palm tree and seashells and a skeleton and treasure chest. Little tiny coins and jewels spilled out of the chest and onto the sand of the island.

"It's all edible except the ship," Diane said. "Brian just loves working in marzipan."

"Brian made this?" I said.

"He finds cake decorating very relaxing," Diane said.

"Wow," I said again.

"This is really something." Amanda was walking around the table, taking the cake in from all sides.

"Brian's very proud of it," Diane said. "I don't know if he'll be able to watch them eat it!" She laughed. The doorbell rang. "Oh, goodness. They're here." She grabbed a handful of eye patches and bandanas from the table in the corner. "These are for you guys." She tossed them at us and went to the door.

I couldn't exactly figure out how to tie the bandana on my head. I knew it was going to totally mess up my hair. All I needed today was bandana head.

"Here," Mallory said. "I'll do it for you."

She came over and stood really close in front of me. She folded the bandana, then reached up and tied it on my head. She stepped back and looked at me, slowly, up and down. "It suits you," she said. She glanced over her shoulder at Amanda. "Doesn't it make his eyes look even bluer?"

"Oh, definitely," Amanda said. She came up behind me and put the eye patch over my head. She adjusted it so it was right over my mouth. "We wouldn't want to hide those eyes."

They both laughed, and I blushed, which made them laugh even harder.

Face painting turned out to be—surprise, surprise—in the bathroom. But all the kids just wanted scars and blood and stuff like that, so it was pretty easy.

I was finishing up the last pirate when Diane stuck her head in. "Aren't you done?" She looked at her watch. "We're running a little behind schedule." If she'd been my mom, I would have said she was getting a little stressed out, but Diane didn't seem like the type of person who got stressed. She grabbed the kid. "Come on, Austin. You don't want to miss the sword fighting."

"But I want another scar!"

"You have enough scars!"

The doorbell rang. Diane groaned. "Get that, okay, Jonah?" She pulled Austin off toward the playroom.

I went and opened the front door. Mr. Decker was standing there, holding a big present.

I don't know why, because seeing him standing there I realized I should have known he'd be there, but I really hadn't been expecting him. I hadn't seen him since that day in his office. I thought he was going to say, "Well, Jonah, did you have that talk with your mother?" But neither one of us said anything. We both stood there, staring at each other. Which was easier for him, seeing as how he had two eyes.

"Well," he said, finally, "this must be the right place."

"I guess," I said. "They're sword fighting in the playroom."

"I'm not surprised," he said, and he moved past me and on up the stairs.

I just stood there, staring out the door at the green lawn and the tulips blooming under the maple tree. Then I closed the door and went upstairs, too.

As I walked into the playroom, a little kid ran up, threw a handful of bread crumbs in my face, and shrieked, "I gotcha! I gotcha!"

The room was filled with little kids, all of them wearing eye patches, bandanas, and nasty scars, and all of them running around throwing bread and screaming.

Mallory was standing in the center of the room, watching Tucker and Austin whack away at each other with long loaves of French bread. Diane, with Cooper clinging to her hip, was shouting, "Go, pirates! Go pirates!" Two kids were rolling around near her feet trying to shove bread down each other's shirts.

I saw Amanda, with a sort-of glazed look on her face, jammed into a corner. Brian was circling the group with a video camera on his shoulder. Kids were jumping up and down in front of him, making faces and trying to get into the picture.

Mr. Decker was standing to one side, still holding the present.

Amanda shoved over beside me. "Fruitcakes," she whispered. "Remember the fruitcakes."

I looked at Mallory. She'd taken off her bandana and eye patch, and her hair shone in the lights of the room. "They're not so bad. Once you get to know them."

Tucker swung his breadstick like a baseball bat, and Austin's breadstick broke off just above his fist. "I won!" Tucker screamed. "I won!"

"*All* the pirates win," Diane said. "Prizes for everybody, first mate."

Mallory started handing out little bags of chocolate coins. She didn't look too happy. I hurried over to help her. After all, it was what we were being paid for.

"Okay, pirates," Diane said, once everybody had their coins, and Tucker had checked to make sure nobody's bag had more than his. "Now. Pirate Amanda and Pirate Jonah are going to lead you on a treasure hunt! Doesn't that sound like fun?"

"But I don't want Jonah," Tucker said. "I want you, Mommy. I want you to come on the treasure hunt!" He started to cry.

"Sweetie." Diane squatted down next to him. "I have to help Mallory with the food. And, anyway, Cooper—"

Tucker threw himself down on the floor, right into all the bread crumbs. "You're always with Cooper. You never do anything with me!"

Mallory groaned. “Here we go.”

“Tucker,” Diane said, but Tucker was screaming and kicking now. The other kids were gathering closer around, like this was much better than bread fights. “Brian, turn that stupid thing off and help me!” Diane sort of shoved Cooper at Brian and knelt down beside Tucker.

“Just wait,” Mallory whispered. “He’ll get his way. He always does.” Her breath tickled against my ear. I kept my head down, in case she wanted to say anything else.

Tucker stopped screaming and kicking. Diane stood up. Her face was flushed, but she was smiling. “Well,” she said. “I guess Pirate Amanda and Pirate Mommy will be leading the treasure hunt.” She looked at me. “I’m going to leave Cooper with you and Mallory, Jonah.”

“I can stay and give them a hand,” Mr. Decker said.

Oh, please, no. Not that.

“No, Dad,” Diane said. “You’re a guest. We have lots of professional help.” She smiled at me. “And Jonah was wonderful with Cooper the other night.”

Brian handed Cooper to me. Cooper grabbed my eye patch and let it snap back against my face.

“See,” Diane said. Then she clasped her hands. “All right, pirates! Outside!”

There was a scramble for the door. Diane was

waving her hand and shouting, "Yo ho ho" as she disappeared into the hallway. Mr. Decker followed her, smiling and shaking his head.

Amanda adjusted her bandana. She looked at me.

"Yo ho," I said.

"Right," she said. And she followed Brian and the camera out the door.

Mallory grinned at me. "Alone at last," she said.

Cooper made another grab for my eye patch. I ducked. "Except for him," I said.

"Cooper," she said, "doesn't count."

CHAPTER FOURTEEN

"What Were You Doing in Here?"

Down in the kitchen, Mallory said, "Just put him on the floor."

"Shouldn't we put him in a pen or something?"

"Diane doesn't believe in playpens." Mallory sighed. "His high chair's in the dining room, but it weighs a ton and a half. He'll be fine on the floor."

I put Cooper down. It was a tile floor, and it looked kind of cold, but he didn't seem to mind. He looked up at me. He was clutching a piece of bread in his right hand. Probably a leftover piece of sword. He stuck it in his mouth and sucked on it.

"Is it okay if he eats that stuff? I think he picked it up in the playroom." I didn't want the kid poisoning himself, when I was supposed to be so great with him.

"Don't worry about it." Mallory sounded exasperated, like I was worrying too much about dumb things. "Cooper will eat dog food if you don't watch him." She was digging around in the cupboards and drawers. "Here," she said. She put a

saucepan and its lid and a bunch of plastic spoons and measuring cups on the floor in front of him.

Cooper took the lid off the pot and dropped the bread inside. Then he put the lid back on. He clapped his hands and laughed. He looked up at us like we were supposed to laugh and clap, too.

I did laugh.

Mallory snorted.

Out the window, I caught a glimpse of Amanda running by. I flipped my eye patch up onto my forehead so I could see better. A pack of five-year-olds was close on her heels. I couldn't hear because the window was shut, but I could tell by the way their mouths were open that they were all screaming. Amanda didn't look too happy.

I turned back to the kitchen. There were packages of hot dogs and buns lined up on the counter. "So. Where do we start?"

Mallory was leaning against the counter. She was smiling that smile. "It's really great to see you again."

I could feel the heat on my face spreading up into my hair. "Yeah," I said. "Me, too. I mean, you, too."

Mallory frowned. She looked almost as great when she frowned as when she smiled. "I was really mad at Stacey the other day. I mean, it was a totally stupid thing to do."

"It was okay." I started to lean against the

counter, too, but it was a little farther away than I expected. I stumbled and had to catch myself. "I was glad she called," I said.

"You were glad Stacey called?" Mallory's eyebrows went up. I loved that, too.

"No, no. I was glad she called because then you called and that was . . . well . . . you know. . . ."

She moved a step closer to me. I could see the blue stuff she'd put on her eyelids.

I took a deep breath. "It was really neat." Good job, Jonah. Even Cooper could talk better than this, and Cooper couldn't even talk. "Talking to you," I said, "was really neat."

She laughed, but it didn't sound like she was laughing at me. It just sounded like a happy sort of laugh. I laughed, too. Her foot sort of sidled over toward mine, and I stepped on it, real fast. She pulled hers back and laughed harder.

She moved closer, and I could feel the warmth of her body. She knocked her shoulder into my side. I bumped back against the dishwasher. The handle jabbed into my other side, and it hurt. I almost said, "Ow!" but I stopped myself just in time.

"No fair," I said instead. "I wasn't ready." I shoved her back, but she'd had time to set her feet, and I couldn't budge her. My shoulder bounced off her shoulder and then came back to rest. I could feel her sweater, scratchy through my sleeve. I could feel the weight of her body, leaning against mine. It was as if the whole universe had condensed down to that spot on my arm that was touching her arm.

She turned, real quick, and, before I knew what she was going to do, she kissed me. Right on the lips.

I really wasn't prepared for *that.* I was still smiling, my lips pulled back tight in this idiotic grin. Her lips pressed against mine. Our teeth banged together, and that definitely hurt. Even more than the dishwasher handle.

Mallory stepped back. She smiled a little bit and looked at me like I was supposed to do something or say something. Should I hug her? Should I kiss her? I didn't think I could risk that. I knew everything there was to know about meiosis and mitosis, and absolutely nothing about what to do after a girl kisses you. I reached my hand up to run it through my hair and realized that I was still wearing the bandana. And the eye patch. My first kiss, and I was dressed like a pirate.

"Oh, no," Mallory said. For a second, I thought she was talking about the way I was dressed. "Where's Cooper?"

The saucepan and the spoons were still in the middle of the floor. The bread was in the doorway to the dining room. Cooper was nowhere to be seen.

There was a loud crash in the dining room.

We both dashed for the door. We got there at the same time, collided in the doorway and bounced back into the kitchen. Then we squeezed into the dining room together.

One of the chairs was lying on its back on the floor. Cooper was sitting in the middle of the table, next to the cake. He leaned over and plucked the pirate ship out of the frosting.

"Cooper!" Mallory screamed.

"No!" I shouted.

Cooper looked back at us over his shoulder. His mouth puckered up. He started to cry. And then, very slowly, he toppled over, right smack on top of the cake.

Mallory put her hands over her face. She slumped against the door frame. "I'm dead," she said into her hands.

Cooper was really screaming now. He'd push himself up, and then his hand would slip in the frosting, and he'd fall down again. He still had the pirate ship, though, clutched in his other hand.

I went over and picked him up. The cake was flattened across the tray it had been on and over the edges, onto the tablecloth. If you looked, you could see the imprints of Cooper's overall buttons in the blue frosting of the sea.

I held him at arm's length. He had frosting in his hair and on his face. He had cake and frosting embedded in his clothes. He even had frosting in the little pocket on the front of his overalls.

I turned him around and held him out, facing Mallory. "What do we do?"

The front door banged open. "Yo ho ho!" Diane shouted. "Hungry pirates to the galley."

Mallory looked like she couldn't decide whether she should pass out or throw up.

I turned to face the door. I was holding Cooper straight out in front of me. He was holding the pirate ship straight out in front of him. He was still screaming.

Diane walked in the door and stopped dead. Then she screamed, too.

I nearly dropped Cooper, who was pretty slippery anyway.

Diane's mouth snapped shut. Then it opened again. Shut and opened. Finally it stopped in the open position. All the little pirates clustered around behind her. Their mouths were open, too. I caught a glimpse of Amanda and Mr. Decker looking at me over their heads.

Brian shoved his way through the crowd. He had the video camera on his shoulder, and the recording light was still on. "My cake," he said. "What have you done to my cake?"

He looked at me, and, for a second, I thought he was going to hit me. I took a step back. There was a chair right behind me. I sat down in it.

Tucker pushed past Diane, too. "It was *my*

cake," he said. He started to cry, too. "Cooper sat right on my cake!"

I was going to say he hadn't actually sat on it, but I didn't think anyone would listen to me.

"This sure is a weird party!" one of the pirates said.

"What did you do?" Diane had got her voice working again. "What were you doing in here?" Her face was the same color as my lobster's had been. I've never seen anybody, not even my own mother, look that mad. "I'm talking to you, Mallory!" Diane said.

Good, I thought. I'd been afraid she was talking to me.

Mallory's hands were hanging straight down at her sides. She took a step into the room. She was crying, but she didn't look sad. She looked almost as mad as Diane. "It wasn't *my* fault," she said.

Everybody looked at me. Diane and Brian and Tucker. Amanda and Mr. Decker and all the kids in the hall. Even Cooper stopped crying, and he sort of craned his neck around to look back at me. "I . . . I . . ." I didn't know what to say. It had sort of been my fault. But not all my fault.

"I come over here," Mallory said. "And you put me to work like . . . like some kind of slave or something." She wrinkled up her nose and her mouth, and her voice came out mean and nasty. "Hand out the prizes, Mallory. Cook the hot dogs, Mallory. Serve the ice cream, Mallory. I have to do everything around here."

I'd been helping, I thought. Or I'd been trying to help. I saw Amanda frowning at me and I stared hard at the back of Cooper's head. He even had frosting on his neck.

Mallory gave a loud sniff and wiped her nose on the back of her hand. She pointed a shaky finger at Brian. "All I ever got was a crummy cake from the grocery store!" She started crying even harder, turned, and ran out of the room. Her footsteps pounded through the kitchen and into the entryway, then on up the stairs. A door slammed, and the house shook.

Nobody in the dining room moved or said a word. Even Tucker and Cooper were quiet.

Mr. Decker pushed his way gently through the kids. He took Cooper from me and handed him to Diane. "You," he said, "take care of this." He took the camera from Brian, turned it off, and put it on the table. He pointed in the direction Mallory had gone. "You take care of *that.*"

Brian left through one door. Diane went out the other, carrying Cooper.

Mr. Decker looked at me. "I don't suppose the hot dogs are ready?"

I shook my head.

"Okay. You're in charge of lunch, Jonah. And get some of this mess cleaned up."

"Okay," I said. I pulled off the bandana and the eye patch and wadded them up on the table.

"What about me?" Tucker said. "I don't even have a cake. How can I blow out the candles if there's no cake?" He looked like he was going to start bawling again.

Mr. Decker bent down. "I thought," he said, "you and I could go buy a crummy cake at the grocery store."

Tucker frowned. "One with lots of little plastic guys?"

"We will find one with so many little plastic guys, you won't be able to see the cake."

"Awesome," Tucker said.

Mr. Decker straightened up and looked at Amanda. "It's a big job, Amanda," he said. He waved his hand at the group of little kids surrounding her. "But I know you can handle it."

Amanda grinned. "No problem. Come on, guys," she said to the pirates. "Let's go watch *Peter Pan.*" They all trooped off upstairs.

As he and Tucker went past me, Mr. Decker patted me on the shoulder. "It'll be okay, Jonah," he said.

I didn't believe him for a minute.

I went into the kitchen and got the hot dogs started. I found a big green garbage bag and took it back into the dining room and cleaned up the cake and the wrecked tablecloth. I set the table. I even found ketchup and mustard and some bags of potato chips. By then, the hot dogs had started to boil. I turned off the heat and went upstairs.

Brian was just coming out of a bedroom when I reached the head of the stairs. He looked at me like he wasn't too sure who I was.

"I just wanted to say . . ." I took a deep breath. "I'm really sorry about your cake."

He nodded. "Where is everybody?"

I explained. "The hot dogs are ready, but I figured we'd better wait for Tucker."

He nodded again. Then he smiled. "It sounds like you have it all under control. I'm going to see if Diane needs some help."

I went into the playroom. The curtains were closed, and it was dark. Only the glow of the TV screen let me see where everybody was. I walked over by the couch, my feet crunching on the bread crumbs. Amanda looked up. She had one kid in her lap and two more pressed against her sides. The rest were jumbled up on the floor at her feet. "It's the exciting part," she said.

I sat down on the arm of the couch and watched Peter Pan zipping around Captain Hook. I knew Amanda was looking at me, but I kept watching the screen. What a crock, I thought. What person in his right mind would want to stay a kid all his life?

CHAPTER FIFTEEN

Really No Big Deal

Mr. Decker and Tucker came back with a big cake covered with plastic football players. "They were all out of pirates," Mr. Decker said.

Tucker didn't seem to mind, and neither did any of the other kids. Diane and Cooper and Brian showed up for the cake and candles, but Mallory never did come back down.

Mr. Decker drove Amanda and me home. I sat in the back seat by myself. Nobody said a word the whole ride, and that was okay. Jonah Truman, Human Disaster, that was me.

Mr. Decker parked in our driveway. He reached into his back pocket and pulled out his wallet. "Brian asked me to pay you guys," he said. He held out two ten-dollar bills.

Amanda looked at the money, then back at me. I shook my head. "I must owe you at least that much for the cake."

Mr. Decker smiled. "Shopping for that cake was one of the best times I've had with Tucker. The best time," he added after a second. He fluttered the bills back and forth. "You guys deserve this."

I shook my head again. "Give it to Amanda. She earned it."

Amanda was staring out the windshield. She shook her head, too. "We're partners," she said. "I'm not going to get paid if you don't get paid."

"Oh, give me a break," I said. "You worked hard. You deserve to get paid."

She twisted around in the seat. "Well, you worked hard, too. Look at all those faces you painted."

"Yeah, but—"

"But what?"

"Never mind," I said.

"You certainly gave Tucker a birthday he'll never forget," Mr. Decker said. "Just having to wear those eye patches and bandanas was worth this much."

"Not to mention the treasure hunt," Amanda said.

"And the bread fight," he said.

He laughed and, after a second, so did Amanda.

She took one of the bills. "Jonah and I will split this," she said. "You keep the other one, Mr. Decker." She opened the car door and climbed out. Then she stuck her head back in. "And remember, if you ever need a job, A & J will be willing to make you a full partner."

Mr. Decker shook his head. "No, thanks. You guys work too hard for your money."

Amanda glanced back at me. I wanted to say something, but I wasn't sure what. "See you later," she said. And she smiled. Then she took off.

Mr. Decker watched her cross the yards and go in her front door. He glanced back at me. "She's a nice girl," he said.

"Yeah," I said. She was a very nice girl. Any other girl would have killed me by now. I nodded toward my house. "Are you coming in?"

"I don't think so," Mr. Decker said. He looked down at his hands on the steering wheel.

"It would be okay." I meant with me, but I couldn't say that. I looked at the face-paint stains on my fingers and the frosting on my jeans. "You know," I said, "I'm probably not going to talk to my mom. I mean, about that thing the other day. That thing in your office."

"I didn't really think you would." I looked up at him. He was staring out the windshield. There was a scab on his cheek where he'd cut himself shaving. "To tell you the truth, I didn't have the faintest idea what to say to you in my office." He looked at me in the rearview mirror. "The situation has never been covered in a workshop."

I noticed there was a hamburger wrapper on

the floor. I stepped on it, and it crunched under my foot. "You did okay," I said, finally.

He laughed. Then he turned around to face me. "I won't talk to your mother, either, Jonah. About . . . well . . . about anything."

I nodded. I opened the door and climbed out of the car. I shut the door carefully; it was kind of an old car. I looked in his window. "You sure about coming in?"

"Yeah." He rubbed his eyes. "I think I'd better go back to Diane's. Maybe I can take Cooper and Tucker off their hands for a little bit. Tell your mom I'll give her a call."

"Okay," I said. "So long . . ." I tried really hard to say "Bob," but I just couldn't do it. "See you," I said instead.

Mom was sitting on the couch, reading a magazine. "Hi," she said. "Wasn't that Bob's car?"

"Yeah. He drove us home." I waved toward the window. "He had to go back to Diane's. He said he'd call."

Upstairs something banged around.

"Liz is taking a bath with her Pretty Ponies," Mom said.

I sat down on the coffee table. "She's probably splashing water on the floor."

"I know. How did the party go?"

The cake got smashed. There was a lot of crying. And I got kissed. "Fine," I said.

"What's this?" She picked a dried blue flake off my knee.

"Frosting." I rubbed my forehead. "I have a headache," I said, and I realized it was true. "It was a really loud party." That was true, too.

"How did Amanda get along with Mallory?"

My stomach tightened. "Okay, I guess. Why?"

She shrugged and sat back on the couch. "Sometimes I feel sort of sorry for Amanda."

Oh, great, I thought. Had Diane called her already? Did she know about me and Mallory? "What's wrong with Amanda?" I asked.

"Oh, I know how hard it must be to be so tall. And not to have any brothers or sisters."

I relaxed a little and thought, Try being short. Try having a little sister. But I just said, "Yeah, I guess."

Mom smiled. "But she's lucky to have a friend like you, Jonah. It's not every boy who'd help her out like this, going to all these parties, and putting up with those little kids." She licked her finger and turned another page of the magazine. "And doing such a good job, too."

I groaned and put my head in my hands. "My head really aches," I said.

She flipped another page of the magazine. "How much did they pay you?"

I opened my eyes and looked into the palms of my hands. "What?"

"Brian and Diane. I was just wondering how much they paid you."

"I think Amanda's got it."

"And you don't know how much it is?"

"No. Well, yeah. It was fine, Mom. They paid us just fine." I didn't dare tell her I was going to let Amanda keep all the money.

Her face had that look it gets when she thinks I should have gotten a higher grade on a paper. "Well, you were over there all afternoon, and Diane told me how much she wanted you and Amanda to do. I know the responsibility you had. . ."

"Mom." It's amazing how she can get worked up about the weirdest things. I thought of all the things I could tell her. And all the things I couldn't tell her. I sighed and ran my fingers through my hair. "Did you know I got into a fight at school?"

Her face sort of froze with the outraged look still on it. "What?" Her voice went up.

"I punched Travis Hunter in the mouth."

She blinked a couple of times. "Jonah Truman," she said, and now she just looked mad at me. "Why in the world would you do that?"

"Jerry said something. And then Travis was a jerk. So I hit him."

"You mean Jerry Fitzner?"

I nodded.

"But you punched Travis?"

"You sort of had to be there." I noticed the magazine had slipped off her lap. I bent down and picked it up.

"Then what happened? Did he hit you back?"

"No. We got sent to the office."

"Bob's office?"

"Yeah." I looked at the picture of some actress and her kid smiling on the magazine cover. "It was weird," I said. "Really weird."

I looked at Mom. She was staring over my head, into the dining room. "I can imagine," she said.

"It's okay now. I mean, it's all worked out."

She looked at me. "What did Bob say to you?"

"He said I shouldn't hit people. And he said I should talk to you."

She closed her eyes, then opened them again. "Well. You can't go around hitting people, Jonah, just because you're upset."

"I know. I won't do it again."

"I hope not."

"Okay."

She looked like she thought she should say something else, but couldn't really think of what it should be. "Okay," she said, finally.

I handed her the magazine. "Are you going to marry him?"

She was staring at the picture of the actress. She sighed. "I really don't know."

I nodded and rubbed at the stains on my fingers. "Do you want to marry him?"

"I don't know that, either." She looked at me. "Does that bother you? I mean, does it bother you that I don't know?"

"No," I said, after a second. What bothers me is when I feel like everybody else knows exactly what's going on, and I don't know anything. "It might bother Liz, though," I said.

Mom ran her fingers through her hair. "I know." She laughed, and her voice sounded more normal again. "I guess it's kind of like all three of us are dating Bob Decker, isn't it?"

"Please, Mom," I said. I made a face. "This is bizarre enough as it is."

She patted me on the knee. "I promise you, Jonah, I'll tell you when I'm thinking about getting married."

"Okay."

The phone rang. I jumped up. "I'll get it." I grabbed it at the desk there in the living room. "Hello?"

"Hi. This is Mallory."

As if I wouldn't know. "Hi." I turned my back so Mom couldn't see my face.

"I just wanted to say . . . well . . . that thing that happened in the kitchen? That was no big deal."

I didn't say anything. There was a mark on the wall where I'd bounced a tennis ball a long time ago.

"I guess I just sort of got carried away. I mean, with the party and everything."

"Yeah," I said. I cleared my throat. "Me, too."

"See. I'm already kind of going out with somebody. Almost, anyway. He's in high school. Tenth grade."

"Oh." And then, before I even thought about it, I said, "Me, too."

There was a little silence on the other end. "Oh," Mallory said. Then, "Is it Amanda?"

"Yeah," I said, and, right when I said it, I knew it ought to be true. "Yeah," I said again, louder.

"Oh, gee," she said. "That's great." Her voice sounded lighter and higher. "You're really cute together, you know. I mean, really cute."

She blew a big puff of air. "I feel so much better. I mean, I'm just so glad we can be friends, now."

Friends? "Yeah," I said. "Me, too."

"Well, I guess I'll be seeing you. Around. Around the house, I mean. I mean, with your mom and stuff."

"Yeah," I said. "I guess."

"Well, bye."

"Bye." And I hung up first. I couldn't believe

I'd said that, that thing about me and Amanda. But, the funny thing was, now that I'd said it, it seemed like I should have said it. And I couldn't figure out why I hadn't said it a long time ago. I shook my head. Nothing today was turning out the way I'd expected.

I turned around. Mom was leafing backward through the magazine. She held up a page. "How do brandied chicken wings sound?"

"Gross. I'm going to change my clothes."

She nodded, and I started up the stairs. I'd change my clothes. Maybe try to fix my hair. Then I'd go over and talk to Amanda Matzinger.

CHAPTER SIXTEEN

"Do You Like Amanda?"

Liz was still splashing around in the tub. She was talking to the ponies, and they were talking back to her. She'd make her voice high or low, depending on which horse was talking. I loved it when she did that. It sounded so goofy.

I wondered what Liz was going to be like when she was thirteen. I wondered if she'd kiss guys in kitchens, and then tell them she was really going out with somebody else. It was sort of depressing, thinking about stuff like that.

I knocked on the bathroom door.

"What?" she said. I could tell she was sitting there, embarrassed that maybe I'd heard her talking to herself.

"When you grow up," I said, "don't kiss guys if you don't really mean it."

She didn't say anything. I just stood there, being really quiet. Then, in a deep voice, she said, "Who was that?" And in a high, squeaky voice, she answered, "That was just Liz's dumb brother."

I laughed, silently, and went into my room. Liz was going to turn out okay.

I pulled off my jersey and wadded it up and tossed it in the corner on top of my horn. Winifred and Dorothy were going crazy, chewing a toilet-paper tube into little bits. I stood there, watching them, and thinking about Amanda. I thought about how nice she'd been to want to help me make money for the trip to the beach. I thought about how she'd been dressing up so much lately, and doing stuff to her hair, and always trying to find excuses to talk to me at school. I thought about a carload of terrorists roaring down the street, and Amanda standing there, right in their path, and me running out . . .

Downstairs the doorbell rang. Then Mom shouted, "Jonah. Amanda's here."

For a second I just stood there, watching the toilet-paper tube get turned into confetti. Then I grabbed the jersey and pulled it back on. I smoothed my hair down, quick, and went downstairs.

Amanda had changed into jeans and a T-shirt. She held up a five-dollar bill. "I got some change. I wanted to give you your share."

I took the money and stuffed it in my pocket. "Uh, thanks, Amanda." I looked at her and thought that maybe she wasn't quite so tall after all.

She looked over my head. "Where's your mom?"

"Upstairs, I think."

She grabbed my shirt and pulled me out the front door onto the porch. "You're a mess," she said, and she wiped her hand on her jeans. Then she crossed her arms and leaned back against the porch railing. "Just what exactly went on at that party, anyway?"

I felt my face getting red. "Well . . ."

"Come on, Jonah. I mean, one minute I'm being chased around the yard by the pack of screaming pirates, and the next thing I know, you've got a kid swimming in the cake. What was going on?"

I nodded. Then I shrugged. Then I nodded again. "It was really, really strange," I said, finally.

She laughed. "That I know."

I went over and sat down on the steps. I hoped she'd come over and sit beside me, but she just kept on leaning against the railing. I had to bend back a little to see her face.

"Mallory kissed me," I said, and my face got even redder.

"She kissed you?" Amanda's voice was a shriek. She put her hands on her knees and leaned forward. "In the kitchen?"

"Amanda." I glanced up at the front window to make sure it was closed. "Not so loud," I said.

She looked at the window, too, then tiptoed

over and sat down beside me. "She kissed you?" she said again.

I nodded. I was glad it was out in the open. Glad she wasn't taking it too hard.

"So what are you going to do now?" Amanda asked. She turned so she was facing me on the step. "I mean, are you going to go out with her?"

"She's already going out with somebody else," I said.

"No kidding? Who?"

"Some guy. Some older guy."

"No kidding," Amanda said. Then she asked, "What was it like? The kissing, I mean."

I thought about it. "Painful," I said. "Our teeth bumped together."

"No kidding," she said, again. She sat up and looked across the street toward the Ehrlichs' house. "I always thought the problem would be noses."

I couldn't even remember where our noses had been. "It was the teeth," I said.

"This may have been worth the five bucks, Jonah." She looked at me. "I'm glad you told me. It's not everybody you can talk to about stuff like this." She smiled, and it was a great smile.

For a second, I thought about leaning over and kissing her, but I decided it might be rushing things a bit. And now I had to worry about noses *and* teeth.

Amanda drew her knees up toward her chest

and wrapped her arms around them. She was staring down at her feet. Her hair sort of swung down against her face, but I could see that she was blushing. "Jonah," she said, and her voice was kind of muffled by her knees. "I have to ask you a really, really important question, and you have to promise to answer it really, really seriously."

I took a breath, held it, and then let it out, slowly. "Okay," I said.

"Do you think I'm . . . well . . ." She leaned over even farther, and I was afraid she was going to fall on her head. "Do you think I'm okay looking?" she said, really fast.

"Yes," I said. "I think you look great."

She let her breath out in a big *whoosh.* She sat up really straight and looked at me. "And do you think I'm somebody that somebody might want to go out with?"

"Yes," I said. Like me, I thought. I'd like to go out with you, Amanda Matzinger. I cleared my throat.

She put her hand on my knee, and I hoped she was going to leave it there. "And do you think Kevin would want to go out with me?"

It was like somebody had hit the remote control, and all of a sudden I was watching another channel. "Kevin?" I said.

"Yeah. Kevin. The guy you're always hanging around with at school?"

"Kevin?" I said. And then, "Kevin Martinez?"

She stood up and walked a little way out into the driveway. Then she turned and walked back. "Jonah. If you think he doesn't like me, you can just go ahead and—"

"No, no." I waved my hands back and forth. "That's not it. That's not it at all." I shook myself, trying to get myself back on track here. Just what was so great about Kevin?

Amanda stood in front of me with her hands on her hips. "Jonah Truman, do you think Kevin would want to go out with me? Just answer me, yes or no."

I looked at her standing there, and the anger faded away. "I don't know, Amanda. Why don't you call and ask him?"

She shuffled her feet. "I can't just call. I want to know first. He probably thinks I'm a total dork or something."

I didn't say anything. I couldn't remember Kevin saying anything in particular about Amanda.

"So would you ask him?" She made a face like she was bracing herself for me to say no.

"I should ask him if he wants to go out with you?"

She shook her head. "No. Just ask him . . . ask him if he likes me."

"That's it?"

"That's it."

I shrugged. "Okay."

"Okay? You'll do it?"

"Sure."

She twirled around with her arms out. Then she stopped, reached over and shoved me back against the next step. "You're a good friend, Jonah," she said. "I mean, I acted really dumb about Mallory, and here you are, calling Kevin for me and everything."

I stared at her. "What about Mallory?"

"I told you that the other day, remember? I told you it was dumb. Getting so mad when you soaked me at the Hennesseys' party?"

"Oh, yeah." She was right. She had told me. I just hadn't known what she was talking about. I felt like I'd spent a lot of time the past few weeks not knowing what anybody was talking about.

She sat down beside me again. "I thought about it, and I think it's okay for us to like other people. I mean, that's the really great thing. That there's no boy-girl stuff with us."

"What does that mean?" I wondered if it made it okay for me to treat her like a guy, but I didn't ask that.

"You know, dating and going out and stuff like that. I think it would ruin everything."

"It would?" A few minutes ago, I'd been thinking it would make everything great.

She put her hands in her hair on each side of her head, like she was trying to press something out of her brain. "Yeah," she said. She looked at me, her head tilted to one side. "It just seems like everything's changing, you know. And I don't want *everything* to change."

"Yeah," I said. That I understood. I looked down at my sneaker.

"Okay," she said. "Okay." She stood up and stretched, long and tall. Her hair caught the sun, and it glowed around her head. "See you." She stopped at the end of the driveway and turned. "Don't forget about Kevin."

I went inside. Mom and Liz were up in Liz's bedroom, doing something complicated with Liz's wet hair. They looked up at me in the doorway.

"Can Kevin spend the night?" I asked.

"I guess."

"Can we rent movies?"

"I guess." She looked up from the braiding. "Bob might come over."

"He can watch, too," I said. I thought about Kevin and Mr. Decker watching movies together and I laughed.

"Oh," Mom said, "I think there may be a message for you. The phone rang, but I let the machine get it."

Liz turned her head as far as she could with

Mom hanging onto the back of her hair. "We think it sounded like a girl," she said.

"Don't get too excited," I said. "She's probably just looking for a friend."

I went back down to the kitchen and played the message.

There was a lot of giggling. Then, "This is Lisa? Lisa from language arts? I'm at Katherine Chang's . . ." There was more giggling. Then, "Katherine really wants you to call her back. At this number."

I wrote the number down. Katherine said something I couldn't hear. They hung up.

I looked at the number. Then I picked up the phone and dialed.

"Hello?"

"Hi, Kevin. This is Jonah. I was wondering if you want to spend the night."

"Oh. Okay. Let me ask my mom." He clunked the phone down.

I thought maybe I should be mad at Kevin or jealous or something. But I wasn't. I guess he couldn't help it if he was irresistible.

He came back in a couple of seconds. "I can come."

"I thought maybe we could rent *Easter Egg Hacksaw Hunt.*"

"Great. I love that movie. Especially the guy in the bunny suit."

I looked at Katherine's number again. "Kev? Do you like Amanda Matzinger?"

There was silence. Then he said, "Yeah. She's okay. I mean, I like her okay."

"Okay. I'll see you later."

I hung up the phone. I went back through the living room and out the front door. I crossed our yard and went up Amanda's driveway and rang the doorbell.

Amanda opened the door.

"He likes you," I said.

"Yes!" she screamed.

I turned and started back for my house.

"Jonah!"

I stopped and looked back.

She was leaning against the door. "Don't forget. We have another job next week. Remember? The circus?"

I pointed my finger at her. "No painting," I said.

She laughed. "I promise. And I'll even wear the clown suit."

"Okay," I said. "I'll be there."

And I walked back home and dialed Katherine Chang's number.